DOWNWARD-FACING DEATH

DOWNWARD-FACING DEATH

A Matt Bolster Yoga Mystery

NEAL POLLACK

THOMAS & MERCER

Text copyright © 2013 Neal Pollack
Originally published as a Kindle Serial, September 2012
All rights reserved.
Printed in the United States of America.

Published by Thomas & Mercer
P.O. Box 400818
Las Vegas, NV 89140

ISBN-13: 9781612187051
ISBN-10: 1612187056
Library of Congress Control Number: 2012945782

For Regina

EPISODE 1

PROLOGUE

———— ○ ————

CASEY ANDERSON'S PHONE ALARM WENT OFF AT 4:00 A.M., like it did every day, except for Sunday, when the electronic harp sounded at five thirty. He didn't particularly like it—no one on Earth enjoyed getting up that early, except for maybe the Dalai Lama, who always seemed content no matter what he had going on—but it was part of Casey's glad sacrifice. He did yoga, and his yoga started before sunrise.

He rolled off the futon low, with minimal sound and movement. His girlfriend didn't have to get up for at least a couple of hours for her practice, and Casey wanted to be respectful of that. At this hour, even her cat didn't budge.

The apartment was about the size and shape of a midsize SUV, with the bathroom and kitchenette separated by a door but sharing pipes. Casey put the teakettle on. Twenty seconds later, he was taking a nice long piss. Then he washed, and flossed, and scraped his tongue with a spoon. Warm globs of white gunk coagulated on the spoon's edge—vulgar toxins that had accumulated while he'd slept. The ayurvedics say that the tongue is a mirror reflection of the health of your organs. When you scrape, you're cleaning your whole system, inside and out. Who was he to argue with five thousand years of accumulated wisdom, especially given the results?

Casey had lost thirty-five pounds in the last year and had shaved his chest. Now he looked like an Olympic swimmer: all bicep, pec, and sinew. His eyes were cue-ball white, and his skin shone like fresh-cleaned stainless steel. Some Sanskrit verses that he didn't understand were tattooed on his right shoulder. Looking at his naked self in the mirror, he thought, *I am fucking beautiful, and I will be forever.* He was young, and not really aware that it was all going to rot away someday.

By then, the water had boiled. Casey filled a tall to-go cup, adding just a couple of squirts of lemon. No caffeine for him, not now or ever again. His body was transmuting into a rigidly tuned system, like a Roman aqueduct or a robot programmed only to serve. He could feel the alchemy all the way down to his nuts. Slipping on a pair of stretchy shorts and a black wifebeater whose center bore an electric-blue image of an unfolding lotus, he took a quick and uncommitted glance at the hot piece of yoga ass sleeping peacefully in his bed, and then he was out the door.

Any other time of day, Casey's commute would have been hellishly clogged, but it was an easy bike ride before dawn. Besides the occasional beer truck, late-night cokehead stragglers were the only real road danger. By now, though, most of them had gone home and passed out. Casey pedaled a couple of blocks down Washington, turning right on Western and then cutting over to Venice, which had a bike lane at least part of the way. The Guatemalan restaurants and payday loan joints quickly gave way to upscale furniture stores and juice bars. Los Angeles may have been a toilet, but at least it was a toilet with all the trimmings.

He passed Crenshaw and bore right at the fork. Just a few doors past the intersection with Pico, he stopped on San Vicente, feeling satisfied at having made the whole trip in less than twenty minutes—easy as homemade, raw vegan pecan pie with almond milk.

He'd arrived at the flagship studio of the Ajoy Yoga empire.

Casey opened the studio every morning. This was his job, except during the full moon. The upward-moving force of *prana* was at its highest on moon days, Ajoy told his students. People felt energetic then but not well grounded, and practicing just filled the head with thoughts of self-importance and invincibility. Of course, that almost directly contradicted Ajoy's traditional instruction; usually he puffed up his students and made them feel like superhumans, avatars of Shiva the Destroyer on Earth. It was a veritable wind farm of ego energy in there most days.

Casey didn't catch the disconnect or the manipulation. Critical thinking had never been his major. Ajoy made a lot of money off guys like him. In lieu of pay, Casey got a free morning class, plus discounts on level-one teacher training in Encinitas, which he was on the wait list for, and, further along, advanced teacher training in Costa Rica, which happened only twice a year and took only forty of the most committed Ajoy Yoga students. It was Casey's fondest dream to unearth the great yoga secrets hidden within the Ajoy pyramid.

For now, he had to organize the pamphlets, chill the for-sale water, desmudge the mirrors. The card swipe on the studio iPad needed to work—that was a new duty, somewhat hard to complete because Casey didn't have a credit card—and the cash register needed tape. He swept up dust clumps whenever they appeared. Most importantly, Casey was in charge of making sure that the folded towels, which by day absorbed Spartan quantities of sweat, didn't smell like warm llama turds. He'd cut into rags any that did.

He got out his keys, but the studio door pushed open to his touch. That was strange, though not unprecedented. The night people sometimes forgot to lock up, which sent no one into a panic. There wasn't much to steal, other than a few rubber plants; several hundred copies of Ajoy's ghostwritten, two-volume autobiography; and a box of coconut-water containers. So Casey moved on in, removing his flip-flops, eyes darting a little to make sure everything was kosher inside.

It wasn't.

The fluorescent lighting flickered weirdly overhead, as though the bulbs had deliberately been replaced with defectives, giving the lobby the feeling of an abandoned mental hospital. A recording played in a loop on the sound system. The music sounded dark and low. A voice, male and deep, chanted:

Ommmmmmmm...Ommmmmmmmmmmm...Ah-ommm mmmmmmmm...

This was the divine sound of universal awareness, the first known utterance from the dawn of time, the ultimate mantra to save those who've been harshly buffeted by life's cruel vicissitudes. But now it sounded as ominous as a visit from the Devil himself. Casey gulped a little.

He noticed a large black arrow, in masking tape, on the floor, pointing toward the big studio. The lights were flickering madly now, almost as if they sensed his presence. The voice that filled the space seemed to grow deeper and louder still.

Ommmmmmmm...Ommmmmmmmmmmm...Ah-ommm mmmmmmmm!

Casey walked, carefully and with excellent posture, toward the big room. He passed through the beaded curtains.

The space was big enough to hold 100 mats, 105 if they squeezed in real tight and ignored the fire marshal's warnings. Someone with a taste for melodrama had placed red cels over the track-lighting bulbs, giving the whole scene the feeling of a charnel house. The chanting continued.

Against the back wall, in front of the mirrors, sat Ajoy's velvet throne. Ajoy would squat there all morning, yelling profanities at the students who weren't doing The Sequence right. Anyone who dared touch the chair without his permission risked banishment from the studio forever. It was Ajoy's most rigid rule. The throne was for him, and him alone.

Casey approached slowly, already starting to sweat from the heat in the room. It was as though he were descending into the bowels of the underworld, where Yama the death god waited, holding his noose and iron rod, preparing to render his inevitable judgment upon us all. Someone definitely was sitting in the chair now.

It was, in fact, Ajoy, though "sitting" might not have been the best way to describe his position. Both his feet had been tucked behind his head, crossed at the ankles. His arms, impossibly, threaded through the gaps created by the folded knees and had been bent behind his back. He was tilted forward slightly, as though he were getting ready to pray, balancing on the phallus that, he liked to brag, could "bench-press five hundred pounds by itself, from a cold squat." The position seemed a little unnatural, even for Ajoy, but his students had seen him perform some strange and amazing physical feats over the years. This might just have been some sort of high-level asana that he did in the mornings, away from the eyes of his admirers.

"Ajoy?" Casey said, but there was no response.

Casey got closer and saw the horror. Something was wrong for sure. Ajoy's eyes were wide, almost like the lids had been glued open, and his tongue stuck out of his mouth much farther than it should have. Ajoy had always mocked *Khechari*, or ritual tongue-cutting, calling it "the last refuge for yoga idiots who are too afraid to face reality." The ritual usually works like this: Over the course of six months, the frenulum, that triangular flesh ridge connecting the tongue to the bottom of the mouth, gets severed a little bit at a time, eventually allowing the yogi to insert the tongue into the hole in the soft palate at the roof of the mouth by turning it backward. According to the *Hatha Yoga Pradipika*, this helps overcome disease, death, sleep, laziness, hunger, thirst, and fainting.

Well, that clearly hadn't worked this morning. Ajoy's tongue flopped down like a dying snail crawled out of its shell. Someone had sliced the frenulum clean through, and quickly, forcing Ajoy's face into a ludicrous parody of lion's breath. But he wasn't breathing, like a lion or otherwise. Ajoy Chaterjee, the wealthiest and most successful hatha yoga mogul in modern American history, was dead.

Lights still flickering and red, mantra still playing sonorously throughout the building, Casey ran from the big room to the lobby so he could call the cops. His first thought was, *I didn't do it*, and of course he hadn't done it, but that was still a phrase that he, as the guy unfortunate enough to discover the body, would have to repeat a lot over the next few days. His second thought, as he picked up the phone, was, *I hope they don't cancel class this morning. My hips feel pretty tight.*

It was possible that they could find a sub.

There were plenty of people in line to claim Ajoy's chair.

ONE

———— o ————

B OLSTER WAS AT THE BEACH. WHERE ELSE SHOULD A MAN GO late on a Tuesday morning after yoga class? He spread out his towel, which bore a yin-yang symbol, on the sand a few feet away from the sidewalk and let the good times wash over him. The day had already brought him a two-hour practice and a juice smoothie so perfectly composed that Bolster practically felt the nutrients oozing from his pores. And now he was stoned, too. All the L.A. bullshit seemed very distant indeed, even though if Bolster turned his head the wrong way, he could pretty much see it behind him. For now, though, it was glorious.

As he lay there feeling totally alive, Bolster felt his skin sizzle pleasantly in the noontime sun. He was average height for a guy, with thick shoulders but hard, trim hips. This gave him plenty of torque if he had to hit someone, which he didn't do these days, at least not often. He had olive-tinted skin that he kept pretty clean, dirty-blond hair that sloped away in the front but was heading toward his shoulders in the back, and three-day stubble. His muscles were defined, but not too much, because he wasn't about maximum effort, in exercise or in life. He'd just turned forty-five, so there was a little pooch, but it was mostly solid underneath the top layer. In another time or setting, he'd be swatting away the women with a tennis racket, but this was L.A., present day, and Bolster was just another pretty-good-looking guy on the boardwalk with a laid-back attitude and a thin savings account. Not that he cared much. Matt Bolster had few attachments.

Bolster's friend Slim stood a few feet to his left, playing the didgeridoo. He wasn't very good; everything sounded like the first few seconds of "Sweet Emotion." Slim had long hair which he kept dirty, a goatee, and a mustache that he greased into curlicues like a silent-film villain. He always wore a long black peacoat, even when it was hot outside, but never seemed to sweat much. Slim was a poet, a mystic, a scholar, and a pretentious bastard. Bolster couldn't have picked a worse wingman if he'd tried. They'd met when Slim was working on a documentary about "underground" yoga teachers, but then Slim had sat on the camera during a Shakespeare festival at the Barnsdall Art Center, and that pretty much took care of the film. Now Bolster was stuck with Slim, who had even less to do during the day than Matt did, not that he minded much. Slim had good weed, and knew where all the bodies were buried.

"Hey, Slim," Bolster said. "Feel like playing something else?"

"Nope," Slim said, and then kept going, making that *whaaa aaaanck whaaaaaaaaaanck* with the didge, which was sounding like an asthmatic pig in heat.

A fully ripped black guy the size of a water tanker, wearing only tight American-flag bikini briefs and wraparound sunglasses, Rollerbladed past on the boardwalk, holding a boom box up to his ear. It was playing the Isley Brothers' "Who's That Lady?" It drowned out Slim for a few seconds. Bolster smiled. It was still the '70s sometimes down here. He loved it. At last, he'd found some peace.

Ten years previous, and the entire ten years before that, Matt Bolster had been an L.A. cop, a good one. Not the best one, because those kinds of superlatives were really hard to gauge, but way better than some, and at least as good as most. He'd started out humping the beat on the hard streets around USC, south of downtown. There had been some tough days for sure. He'd gotten kneecapped with a piece of plywood and needed minor surgery. But there'd also been a lot of easy apartment-break-in work and the occasional available coed with a fetish for a man in uniform. Bolster had handled that gig well.

But then he got transferred to Crenshaw and his situation seriously declined. He saw things he didn't like: hookers with their throats slit; kids sleeping on mattresses on the floor, five to a room, smuggled cocaine stuffed into their pillows; an endless army of dogs, branded like cattle, snarling at ruined fences, hungry for freedom and human flesh. He began to feel like the city was killing itself, one block at a time, and he couldn't do anything. The drinking didn't help, either, and there was a lot of that, often all night, at cop bars and dive bars and Jumbo's Clown Room and the occasional Hollywood underground lounge and rehabbed downtown hipster joints like the Golden Gopher. Bolster had thrown back great streams of scotch and bourbon and gin, often paid for by the house because he'd flashed his badge. Then sometimes chicks would show up with pills and things would get *really* intense. One night he hooked up with these three hairdressers and they did some blow and horse tranquilizers and then it was five thirty a.m. and the sun was rising and he was standing on Figueroa shirtless and he couldn't move his feet. It felt like he had gravity boots on.

Two days later, Bolster made detective.

That didn't make him any happier. Sure, he got to spend more time at a desk and less time chasing parole-jumping Avenues affiliates down hot, dusty hillsides in Lincoln Heights, but it was still the same cesspit of a town. Nothing got done. The mayor hired a gang-prevention czar who was actually still in a gang. Every week, the Korean Mob dumped a headless problem gambler into an untrawled culvert. Bolster started drinking at his desk. He slept late and called in, saying he'd been on a stakeout.

Still, he solved some cases and got promoted. He took a bribe from a pit boss at the Commerce Casino and didn't tell anyone.

Sleep didn't come easy. When it did overtake him, Bolster ground his teeth to nubs. He began to get weird pains in the sides of his neck and in his temples. His legs tightened, he got a gut, he got slow. Boners flew only half-mast, if at all. He put his fist through a car window and needed stitches. He was declining fast.

This girl Bolster had been screwing every other weekend invited him to a yoga class at the Hollywood YMCA. "I think it'll be good for you," she said. Of course, a lot of things *would have* been good for him, but that didn't mean he did them. The whole point was that Bolster wasn't taking care of himself, because he hated himself and you don't take care of something you don't love. Still, she was a fine piece with strong thighs, and she could also hold a conversation. Bolster's life at that point was marked by declining assets, and this was one asset he wanted to keep around for a while. So he went to yoga class.

He didn't know what to expect, but he got something pretty normal. A kind-looking woman—not too young and not too skinny, and wearing a bandanna around her head so she looked like the lady worker in those You Can Do It! posters that used to be popular—had them all lie on their backs in a wood-floored room about half the size of a basketball court. In fact, it may even have *been* half a basketball court. There were maybe twenty-five people in the room, which seemed like a lot, but Bolster later learned that was about average size for a popular L.A. yoga class. Bolster's mind was twitchy, but he tried to be respectful. He wriggled around on his back, feeling like a tipped-over keg at a party.

The teacher had them all place their left hand three inches below their belly button. From there, it was breathing instruction: Inhale from the pit of your abdomen, all the way up to the top of your head. Exhale, reverse, without opening your mouth. They lay there for five minutes, by the end of which Bolster could hear himself snoring. The practice hadn't even started yet.

Then they were up and doing poses. The ones where they had to bend forward and deep, Bolster couldn't accomplish so well. If the poses required a little muscle, he was better. He sweated a lot, even though they weren't moving very fast. Bolster later learned that was because his body contained substantial toxins; five years later, when he was exercising a lot harder, he sweated a lot less. And they weren't just physical toxins, either. Yoga philosophy talks about a phenomenon called *samskara*, or negative sense impressions that cause suffering. Well, Bolster had been through a tough decade. His *samskara* count was high. He needed to focus on his breath for a while.

When it was over and they descended into *savasana*, or corpse pose, Bolster felt a little tingle at the base of his spine, and then he wasn't thinking anymore. When the teacher rang the bell, he snapped into consciousness, feeling more awake than he had in a while.

He wanted to do the yoga again.

Afterward, his girl introduced him to the teacher, whose name was Rhonda.

"Matt Bolster," Bolster said.

"Seriously?" said the teacher.

"What?"

"You just took a yoga class and your name is Matt Bolster?"

"Yeah."

"Don't you get it?"

"No."

"You will."

He got it soon enough. When his parents christened him Matthew Bolster back in 1967, they had no idea that they were dooming him to a future where their son would share both his first and last names with popular yoga props. Back then, yoga was something that the Beatles did in India, not something offered at your neighborhood gym alongside Zumba and water aerobics.

Yet soon, there Matt Bolster was, doing yoga every Saturday morning. The girl moved to Seattle, but he got a membership at the Y and started going twice a week. He stopped drinking as much and started craving that high he felt after class instead. Driving back to his apartment, he'd feel clear and open and happy. The good feelings would fade after a while, usually by the next day, but now that Bolster knew how to get to that place in his mind, he wanted to go back all the time.

After a while, the classes at the Y were too easy for him. Not physically, so much, but something else was lacking, something more substantive. He began to suspect that a deeper truth lay at the heart of this yoga thing, and he wanted to seek out that truth, to find it in himself and others. Fortunately, a studio in his neighborhood was offering a deal: ten classes for seventy bucks. Enlightenment awaited him at a bulk price.

Bolster was thinking about all this as he lolled at the beach while Slim played the didge. He took a sip of ice water, which he'd flavored with sliced cucumbers, and pulled his phone out of a bag. It was time to check his Twitter feed.

Big mistake.

His Twitter feed had exploded in the last hour. Apparently, the body of Ajoy Chaterjee had been found in his flagship studio on San Vicente, contorted and mutilated into horrible shapes. Already, people were making jokes about how this was part of Ajoy's "advanced series," and that thought occurred to Bolster as well. How could it not? The term "finishing pose" also came to mind. But then this sentence in a *Huffington Post* story caught Bolster's attention: "The LAPD has no leads, no suspects, and few clues."

"Shit," Bolster said.

"What?" said Slim.

"Ajoy's dead."

"Chaterjee? Did his ego explode?"

"No, he was murdered, apparently," said Bolster.

"Whoa," Slim replied. "Heavy."

"Who would do that?"

"Who wouldn't?" said Slim. "A lot of people had it out for Ajoy. That guy was nasty."

"Yeah, but murder?"

"They try to warn us when we start practicing," Slim said. "Don't get attached. Don't trust your gurus. But then, before you know it, you're following your meditation teacher up to Mendocino and he's asking you to monitor his pot farm for three months while he goes on silent retreat in Thailand."

"That doesn't happen to everyone, Slim," Bolster said.

"Whatever," said Slim. "Yoga's a sleazy business, Matt. You know that as well as anyone."

Bolster did, but he wished he could forget. That bit about the cops not having any clue, while not surprising, meant that he was probably going to have to work today, which was a shame because he was pretty high.

Sure enough, even as he had that thought, his phone rang. He answered it.

"Bolster?" said the voice on the other end.

"That's me," Bolster said.

"We need your fucking help."

TWO

———— o ————

Y EARS EARLIER, BEFORE HE QUIT THE FORCE, BOLSTER started going to yoga studios. In particular, he took an interest in this one up in Los Feliz, which was small and neighborhoody. He loved the dark walls, the blond wood, the soft lighting, the intoxicating smell of incense and girl sweat, and the fact that he could go in there and no one would judge him if he stumbled a little or cried softly to himself during *savasana*. He started taking classes several days a week. Some weeks he'd go every day, even if the classes involved nothing more than old ladies doing seated twists and chanting off-key hymns to Gaia.

His fellow cops gave him shit, calling him "yoga man," "Gandhi," and way worse. One morning, he opened up his locker to find a pair of dance tights inside. Another, he got an exercise mat with a picture of a vagina taped to the center. This was before the LAPD started offering yoga classes as part of its fitness program. Bolster tried to tell the guys that yoga was for men, too. All kinds of athletes did it. Diamond Dallas Page, the former pro wrestler, was a yoga teacher in Hawaii, for fuck's sake. They weren't having it, but Bolster didn't care. He loved yoga.

The next time he had vacation, he found himself signing up for a two-week retreat at a yoga center in Tulum, just south of Cancún on Mexico's Yucatán Peninsula. This was a serious deal, not some ordinary yoga for pikers. People traveled from all over the world for this. Bolster did *asana* three times a day; ate an organic, vegan diet; and swam in the shadows of Mayan ruins. He felt cleansed, whole, and, for the first time in forever, really glad to be alive.

In the evenings, they'd all get together in the *sangha* to meditate and listen to the teacher talk about yoga philosophy. Yoga had ancient roots, the teacher said, devised thousands of years ago by people wiser than you or me to help relieve humans of the burden of their inevitable suffering. We all suffer, without exception, and yoga understands that.

Yes, Bolster thought.

But it also accepts us, and loves us without judgment, despite our suffering. When we practice yoga, we're really practicing kindness and compassion. Our true selves are illumined in that kindness, in the all-seeing light of pure awareness.

Oh, yes.

Bolster felt himself being lifted up into some sort of ecstasy that he didn't understand. It was as though a shaft of mystical energy were bursting from his heart, filling the universe with unlimited joy. He felt so good, it almost hurt. Was he joining a cult? Who knew? And who cared? *Magical yoga powers!* he prayed to himself, though maybe not quite in those words. *Transcend me to another realm!*

"Just don't get attached," said the teacher, "because it's all temporary."

The teacher is wrong, Bolster thought. *I'm going to feel this way forever because I'm a beautiful creature of the universe. Yoga will sustain me.*

Bolster went home, quit the force, and, using his cashed-in city pension money, put down a deposit on a two-hundred-hour yoga teacher training program. At last, he thought, he could put the evil city and all its troubles behind him and float trouble-free in a world where everyone is kind and generous and good.

That's not exactly how it played out.

Matt Bolster became a yoga teacher, and no one gave a shit. It's not like you could just hang up your shingle and then rich people would come to you seeking enlightenment. Well, it happened like that occasionally, but usually to hot chicks who actually took the time to design some sort of business plan and *asana* system. Not to him.

He moved down to Venice, into a studio apartment above a low-rent pot dispensary run by the Russian Mob. None of the local studios were hiring, and his search for private clients went poorly. He got one class a week at a "donation" studio, but the students were all out-of-work actors and he was lucky to take in fifty bucks when it was all over. The only other gig he could get was a Sunday-morning class with an AA group, but he didn't charge them. He'd never twelve-stepped himself, but he knew what they were feeling all too well.

The money started to run out, so Bolster looked elsewhere for support. Living a monastic life in contemporary Venice gets expensive. Rents are high. You need a car. Let's face it: you need a smartphone, too. Juicing your own food isn't cheap. Bolster had overhead.

Mostly, he took on ticky-tacky work: missing persons, the occasional cheating-spouse stakeout, credit-card fraud—stuff that could be polished off quickly and easily. He stayed out of the murder game, though; it was a dark and poisonous path, and he didn't want to get sucked back into the maw. But sometimes cases came calling anyway. There was a surprising amount of yoga crime in L.A. The cops had no idea what to do with any of it.

So that's how Bolster came to be sitting at a Greek diner on Santa Monica, nursing a green tea with lemon, across from the LAPD's own Esmail Martinez, the guy who'd once put the "vagina mat," as it was now known, in his locker. Martinez had been acting out of ignorance, not real malice. Now was Bolster's chance to not only forgive but make some real cash, too. Profits are the best redemption.

"Thanks for meeting, Matt," Martinez said.

"I made the time," said Bolster. "Which is tough to do when you've got clients."

"You don't have any clients."

"How do you know?"

"Because you don't. Because you're a fucking yoga detective."

"Fair enough," Bolster said. "So, what've you got for me?"

"You're familiar with Ajoy Chaterjee, right?"

"I am."

"And you probably know he was found murdered this morning."

"I do."

"It was real sick, too. Someone cut the bottom part of his tongue, and it was hanging out of his mouth like he was a frog trying to catch flies."

"*Khechari*," Matt said.

"Did you just sneeze?"

"It's an ancient Vedic tongue-cutting ritual designed to help ward off disease or death."

"See, I didn't know that," said Martinez. "I thought it was just garden-variety mutilation. That's why you're useful."

"Whoever did it was being ironic. That's what passes for a joke in yoga-land."

"Huh. The body got all fucked up, too. It looked like all his joints were pulled out of their sockets."

"Interesting details," said Bolster. "But you tell me like you think I should care."

"We figured you might know something, or know someone who does."

"Nope. My world and Ajoy Yoga's never crossed. It's like saying, 'Hey, you're a Catholic, so you must know who killed the pope.'"

They regarded each other uncomfortably as a Katy Perry song played over the diner's sound system—a terrible music choice under any circumstance, Matt thought.

"Be that as it may," Bolster said, "I could probably help you out."

"Well, fucking good for you," said Martinez.

"And I assume you're hiring, unless you really just wanted to buy me lunch."

"We can pay you five now and forty-five if you give us something we can use."

"Forty-five?"

"Thousand."

Bolster tried to keep his poker face, which was hard to do, considering that "Poker Face" was now playing over the sound system. Fifty grand could get you through almost nine months of living in Los Angeles, assuming you were careful and you mooched other people's weed most of the time. *Man*, Bolster thought, *if you're patient and respectful, the universe really does provide you with what you need.*

"That's a lot of money, Esmail," Bolster said. "Isn't the city broke?"

"We got a fund," said Martinez.

"But fifty grand? Shouldn't you be giving that to a community center in Boyle Heights or something?"

"Bolster, nobody gives a fuck about Boyle fucking Heights. Now, are you going to help us solve this bitch or not?"

"Such a kind offer," Bolster said.

"Look, man, I don't want to work with you, either, but we don't know shit about this yoga world and we need someone who can get deep into it."

"I'm your guy."

"Good."

They shook hands.

"You wanna give me a ride down to the scene?" Bolster asked. "I took the bus here."

THREE

—————— o ——————

THE FREAKS WERE OUT ON SAN VICENTE, MOURNING THEIR guru. Police tape and flashing lights hadn't stopped them from laying out wreaths and bouquets and garlands and candles and little bowls of dried rice. Someone had taken a mannequin, put a photo of Ajoy's face on the head, and placed the arms and legs in a crucifixion pose. People were doing Ajoy's trademarked sequence on the sidewalk, and others played the guitar and sang, despite the fact that Ajoy hated most music and never allowed it in his studio. "Yoga is about strength," Ajoy once told the *LA. Times*, "and music is about weakness. Except for Michael Jackson, who is a friend. I taught him all the yoga he needed in two days."

And now look. They were both dead.

There were certainly plenty of cameras around, both professional and Instagrammatical. This Big Hollywood Death warranted coverage, at least for a couple of days. TMZ had put itself at the center of the scene, promising an inside look at Ajoy's sleazy yoga empire, but thus far hadn't revealed much other than the fact that Ajoy had once gone to George Clooney's house for dinner and sometimes gave private lessons to Gigi Grazer and Julianne Moore. Everyone had seen the pictures of Ajoy at the Hollywood fund-raisers. He always wore the flashiest suits and had the brightest smile.

Bolster, with Martinez trailing, moved through the crowd like an arrow slicing air. No one recognized him or cared who he was. He hoped it stayed that way forever. Besides, if you took your yoga practice to its extreme, which he tried to do, the self didn't exist anyway. What's the point of gossiping about a ghost? Bolster ducked under the crime-scene barrier, opened the door, and went inside to see what he could see.

A couple of cops were milling around, not doing much. Everything had been covered in plastic. The lights were on at full brightness. People like to pretend that where they practice yoga is some kind of sacred space, but the word *shala*, which everyone assumes means "studio," actually translates to "barn" in Sanskrit. Nothing is holy, and everything is, which is quite a paradox. Regardless, it's amazing how quickly a yoga studio can turn into a quarantine zone.

A good-looking kid, maybe twenty-three years old, was sitting in a folding chair. Other than a little fear and a lot of exhaustion, there was emptiness behind his eyes. Yoga had stripped him of his personality and replaced it with absolutely nothing—if there'd ever been anything there to start. Bolster felt confident. He was fluent in Bro.

He pulled up a chair alongside, and straddled it manlike, extending a hand.

"Hey, dude, what's up?" he said. "My name's Matt."

"Casey," said the bro.

"So, you've probably had a pretty tough day."

"Yeah," said Casey. "And I didn't get to do my practice, so I'm pretty stressed out."

"I hear you, man," Matt said. "So, listen, I'm working with the cops here, and"—he lowered his voice—"*I know they're kind of douche bags.*"

Martinez rolled his eyes.

"But maybe you could tell me a little bit about what you saw this morning."

"I could do that," Casey said. "You seem cool."

"Oh," said Bolster. "I am the *coolest.*"

Now Martinez looked like he was having a seizure. Still, Bolster got the rundown. Casey seemed bored by the story, as though he'd told it a hundred times that day, which he probably had, but Bolster coaxed him. As Casey talked, Matt sat there with his mouth practically open. There were plenty of telling details: the red cels on the overhead lights, the melodramatic chanting on the sound system, the fact that Chaterjee's limbs had been broken into a ludicrous parody of *asana*. Even the black arrow on the floor, as though this were some sort of middle-school haunted house, screamed Hollywood pretension. This wasn't some sort of cash-register holdup or business deal gone wrong. A normal person would have plugged Ajoy once in the brain or cut his throat and then have been done with it. No, this murder had been meant as a kind of *show*, put on by someone with a twisted goal. The whole thing had been destined for discovery, to be played over and over again in a tabloid loop, like some sort of fabled lesson. Otherwise, why go to all the effort?

"You got anything else for me, Casey?" Bolster asked.

"Ajoy's tongue," Casey said. "I didn't know tongues were that long."

"They can be."

"It was flopped way down. There was some blood on his chest."

"Rough."

"I'm gonna have nightmares."

"I bet, man."

"And I'm gonna have to find another teacher."

"Be your own teacher," Bolster said. He wanted to slap himself as soon as he did, because he knew that was total crap.

"OK," Casey said. He wasn't listening anyway.

"Casey, did you touch the body or the chair?"

"Just the door and the phone."

"No other prints?" he asked Martinez.

"Nothing."

"Who would have been the last person in the studio before you?"

"The night class can be pretty light, so sometimes the teacher handles the desk, too."

"Who taught last night's class?"

"The schedule says someone named Chelsea Shell," Martinez said. "We're looking for her."

"Chelsea is awesome," said Casey. "Her classes are really crazy."

"I bet," said Bolster.

Craziness was the last thing Bolster wanted out of life, or yoga. But he had a feeling that things were going to be challenging for the next few weeks. He just needed to do what his training taught him: to observe without judgment.

"Martinez," he said, "this guy doesn't know anything else."

"Thanks for telling me," said Martinez. "But we might hold him here for a while."

"I've got to ask straight out, buddy."

"OK," Casey said.

"Did you kill Ajoy?"

"Hell, no," Casey said. "I loved Ajoy. He was the shit."

"You got any plans to skip town?"

"Why would I do that?"

"Let him go," Bolster said.

Martinez ran a hand over his face.

"Jesus," he said. "All right."

"That's awesome," Casey said, looking relieved. "I was hoping to get to a three thirty Power class in Santa Monica."

"Enjoy," said Bolster.

Casey dashed out the door like a spaniel puppy unleashed in a dog run.

"Man, I wish I were young and stupid," Bolster said.

"Well, you've got half of that nailed down," Martinez said.

"You're funny," said Bolster.

Matt spent the next half hour combing the studio, taking pictures with his phone. It was just a foyer with a desk, cubbyholes, and a water dispenser connected to a big, empty room, which also contained small male and female changing areas separated by a curtain. A barely working toilet sat next to a sink in a side closet. Ajoy would have left that last part out if it had been legally allowable. Even though he was as rich as Weinstein, Ajoy hadn't gone in for softness and frippery. His studio wasn't a place for healing. He'd wanted to break people down. Apparently, he'd broken someone too far.

But it also wasn't really a place where a murder could easily take place, Bolster thought. There was too much open space, and it was too easy for someone to get away, especially someone as fit and powerful as Ajoy Chaterjee. Bolster had a theory—and it was only a rudimentary working one at this point—that someone had done their damage to Ajoy ahead of time and had brought him into the studio prekilled. This wasn't like a glazed duck hanging from a window in an Alhambra Chinese barbecue joint; the meat hadn't been cured in-house.

Martinez was right beside him, like some kind of government minder. It pissed Bolster off. But Bolster knew that wasn't a healthy emotion, so he observed it, appreciated it for what it was, and let it go. He had what he needed for now.

"Let me know if you hear anything about this Chelsea Shell," he said.

"Same," said Martinez.

"It's got to start there."

"Obviously. She's supposed to teach tonight."

"Yeah, but I'm guessing class is canceled," Bolster said.

Bolster went outside. Cars lurched past as people went unthinkingly about their precious business. It was late afternoon, a little after four, and the day had already started to cool down—one of the benefits of living in this humanity-choked corner of the planet.

Bolster felt a little uneasy about the scene in the studio, but it wasn't like some previously unknown perversion of human nature had been revealed. At least not yet. He'd seen a lot of darkness in his days, and it was hard to surprise him.

Even a yoga murder didn't seem strange. Yoga served as a magnifier of passion, making everything more intense, bubbling all the *samskara* to the surface, until everyone was an open wound. Now Bolster just needed to identify the right people, and the right passions, and then he'd have fifty grand in the bank—fifty-one if you counted the thousand that was already there.

○

Bolster went home, got on his computer, and did clip work. There was a lot of information on Ajoy Chaterjee.

According to all accounts, Ajoy was born in Howrah, a large industrial city in West Bengal, sometime in the late 1940s. His father, a middle-class accountant, was also a sometime practitioner of the yogic arts, but commercial considerations and a lazy constitution had stalled his progress. For Ajoy, he determined a more drastic fate.

Legend told that Ajoy's father, when the boy was only four, wrenched him away from the loving arms of home and placed him in the hands of Sri Charan Jindra, a master of the Vedic arts who taught a select group of pupils under the Great Banyan tree in the Indian Botanic Garden. Ajoy sobbed and pleaded for his mother and beloved grandmother, but his father knew that this child was destined for something higher, for a state of mental being beyond the puerile attachments of family, country, ethnicity, caste, and simple conceptions of the self. There was so much suffering in the world, and Ajoy's father wanted him to have no part. The guru took the boy in exchange for a hundred rupees and a mélange of spices, many of which he said were lacking in his own kitchen. Thus began Ajoy Chaterjee's yoga education.

Here, Bolster realized as he researched, Ajoy's story began to resemble the narrative of a kung fu movie. He saw a few possible reasons for this similarity. First, all martial arts origin stories—and yoga was definitely a distant cousin of the martial arts, as evidenced by the popular '70s flick *Kung Fu vs. Yoga*—sounded similar. Also, it was quite possible that Ajoy had made a lot of it up to satisfy the hungry word counts of the dozens of journalists who interviewed him every year. The details were constantly shifting, but Bolster couldn't figure out if that was because of the incompetence of the interviewers, because Ajoy was playing with them, or if it was a little bit of both. Finally, and Bolster knew this truth well, yoga apprenticeship is hard when you're an adult and all the ego structures are in place, needing to be broken down one brick at a time. He often wondered, as did many passionate practitioners, what life might have been like if he'd started young, before he began to have real problems. Ajoy was a test case.

It was said that Sri Charan Jindra knew eight thousand *asana*, perhaps one-tenth of what *his* master, a goat farmer in a remote Himalayan village, had taught him nearly four decades prior. Of those eight thousand, he taught eight hundred to his five students, including Ajoy Chaterjee, in twenty series of forty poses each. Each sequence built on the next, though not necessarily in degree of difficulty. Some series involved little more than prone breathing with the arms and legs arranged in various stages of rest, while others were composed of preposterous arm balances and fiendish inversions. There were simple twists and impossible contortions, great feats of strength and endurance, and many moments of quiet. Because Jindra accepted no beginning student over the age of five, none of them had the attitude of "I can't do this." They didn't know what was possible or what wasn't. They just did.

For eight years, Ajoy studied under the kind guidance of Sri Charan. They did poses all morning, and then they sat under the banyan tree, eating sweets and drinking mango juice, as Sri Charan taught them Sanskrit from the original texts, using the original Vedic chants. Ajoy learned to sing the Gita and the *Mahabharata*; thrilled to the exploits of the magnificent Hanuman, the monkey god who served humankind with strength and wit; and listened, with only moderate comprehension, as Sri Charan sang the Upanishads, one after another, to his loving pupils. They meditated quietly in the shade of the great tree. In the rainy months, they'd retreat to a *shala*—literally, a room next to a barn—where their studies would continue.

Once a month, Ajoy's parents would visit and he'd perform songs and poses for them. At first, they were thrilled to see him, and he them, but as the years moved along, though his joy only increased in their presence, they grew more and more wistful, which surprised him because he was growing more peaceful and stronger by the day. He'd achieved his father's dreams of yogic bliss, and couldn't understand why they were separating from him.

Ajoy found out soon enough.

One morning, as legend had it, or at least as Ajoy told it, Sri Charan's students awoke under the tree to find their guru gone. They waited for him to bring them breakfast, as he always did, but he didn't come. They practiced their *asana* uneasily, in silence. At noon, a cart appeared, driven by two strong, unsmiling men. One by one, they took the children, bound their hands and feet, and threw them, sobbing, into the back of the cart. They took a rough three-hour ride to Kolkata, to one of the most wretched neighborhoods imaginable. The men then untied the children and left them standing in a sewer.

For the next eight years, exactly the amount of time he'd existed in Sri Charan's idyllic paradise, Ajoy would wander the streets of Kolkata, begging for food and change. He started off working in teams with his fellow schoolmates, but the cruel vicissitudes of life gradually parted them. For a while, Ajoy supported himself by working in a *chaat* shop, living in a room in the back along with a half dozen other employees. His feet grew raw and stained with filth.

And yet, every day he'd find an open space to practice his poses and to meditate—no matter how hungry and tired he felt. He didn't abandon his yoga for anything. Even if the other students didn't realize it, Ajoy understood early on that this was a test, part of his training. When the Buddha left his father's cosseted palace for the first time, he saw an old man, he saw a sick man, and he saw a dead man. At that point, he realized the same fate awaited him someday. Even the most exalted among us must die.

Sri Charan wanted his students to understand that life wasn't easy for anyone, that suffering was universal. Anyone can be a yogi in times of pleasure and abundance. But the true test comes in times of hardship.

This realization didn't make Ajoy hate his guru any less for abandoning him on the shoals of adolescence. He lost his virginity to a cheap courtesan, and he lost the most virile years of his youth to want and desperation. As he read this, Bolster thought, *I spent my teenage years going to keggers in the desert. Ajoy spent his sweeping shit out of the gutter.*

Bolster looked at his phone. It was almost six p.m. He needed to meet his source.

FOUR

○

BOLSTER SAT OUTDOORS AT A CAFÉ ON ABBOT KINNEY, drinking an iced mint-yerba-maté latte. Maybe it wasn't the traditional private eye's evening drink of choice, but he'd already boiled his liver enough through the years. Now he tried to keep it clean, save for the occasional glass of wine with dinner. Sometimes if he got really baked, he'd drink a couple of beers, too. Then again, who cared? He knew one yoga teacher who drank two double Bloody Marys before her Sunday *vinyasa* flow class at Brentwood Bodyworks. Whatever gets you through the hours.

Suzie Hahn pulled up on her little powder-blue scooter, yoga mat bungeed to a plastic milk crate on the back. She saw him immediately and gave a wave.

"Hi, Matt!" she said.

Bolster stood up to greet her, and she gave him a limp hug, her usual fare. He shouldn't have been surprised, but he always was, because yoga people were big on the hugging, like they'd never see you again after they let you go. Not Suzie, though. You'd *always* see her again.

"I got your text and I came right over," she said. "I was on my way to the Lotus Leaf to take Dave's six thirty restorative class. Do you know Dave?"

"No," Matt said.

"Oh, he's really good. Quite natural. I was having trouble deciding between him and Patricia Robinson, who's got a new donation flow class at the Wellness Bar behind the Ed Hardy store. My African-dance *vinyasa* workshop went long, and I wasn't sure if I'd be able to get over there in time, but then your message came around and I thought, you know what? I've already taken six yoga classes in the last two days, and that's probably enough."

"Well, I appreciate it," Bolster said.

"Sure!" Suzie said.

Suzie Hahn kept a blog called *Yoga Happens* that no one really read, but that didn't stop her. All she did, all day long, was take yoga classes. Also, sometimes she took Pilates. She usually got in for free because the teachers were desperate for whatever publicity they could get, however slight. If it was yoga and it was anywhere within thirty miles of Downtown Los Angeles, sometimes farther, Suzie was there. Matt sometimes wondered how she kept it going—or even why—but her enthusiasm and energy never seemed to flag, and she never seemed to get hurt. She'd been doing it forever and had looked like she was twenty-seven years old since she was actually twenty-seven, which was a long time ago now. She didn't seem to have an actual job. When Matt, on occasion, asked her how she paid her bills, she was always very cryptic.

"By the way," Suzie said, "I never got to tell you how much I enjoyed your free class at the AA center last week."

"Thanks," Bolster said. "I can't believe you actually went."

"Well, I was trying to choose between that and Shira Weiss's level two at the Dharma Loft, but then I thought about it and I realized, when was I going to get the chance to take a class given by an ex-cop?"

"I teach every week," Matt said.

"Right. I know! And that's awesome."

"So, listen," he said, "I got called in to help on the Ajoy murder."

NEAL POLLACK

"Oh my God!" she said. "You'll be perfect for that!"

She used a tone like she was congratulating a friend on getting a really good job, which didn't seem all that appropriate to Bolster. But he let it go.

"Did you see my post about it this afternoon?" she asked. "I put it up as soon as I heard."

"Missed it," Bolster said. "Tell me."

"You know, I used to take Ajoy's morning class every day before things got weird at the studio."

Suzie always said something useful if you directed her right.

"What do you mean, 'got weird'?"

"Well, for ages it was always a big party in there. Intense, but fun. Like, when Ajoy got hot, everyone wanted to come to class, and he just soaked it all in because he knew he had something. Then, about a year ago, Ajoy really started yelling at his students a lot, calling them rich, spoiled idiots, telling them he was going to teach them a real lesson. He was saying stuff like, 'When I die, what are you going to do then? How's your yoga going to look?' It was super creepy. There'd be, like, these fifteen-minute *savasana*s where he'd play music like what you'd hear at a morgue, and then he'd sit on his throne and pretend to sob and blow his nose like he was at a funeral."

"Whoa."

"I know, right? Sometimes students would be in the middle of practicing a tough pose and he'd pull their mats right out from underneath their feet. And then he'd mock them when they fell down. Everyone was really off-balance all the time."

"Why the change?" Matt said.

"I'm not sure," Suzie said. "He just kind of…snapped. And it kept getting worse."

"That's weird," Matt said.

"Yeah."

"So, what about this teacher named Chelsea Shell?" he asked.

"I know Chelsea," Suzie said. "I even knew her before she was teaching. There's a story with that one, all right."

30

The waitress came over.

"Can I get you anything?" she asked.

"Nothing for me," Suzie said.

"It's on me," said Matt.

"Are you sure?"

"Of course."

Without hesitation, Suzie said, "Can I get a double farmer's salad with the dressing on the side, and that tomato-feta tart?"

Suzie looked at Bolster. "I haven't eaten all day," she said.

That, thought Bolster, *is how it's done.*

Over some iced refills, Bolster had to listen to Suzie tell him how she'd been going to a lot of *kundalini* classes in Hollywood to help her get over some "emotional blockage," and that there was this new "420 yoga" class in Atwater Village that he should try out because she knew he liked pot. Atwater Village seemed pretty far away to him, especially in late-afternoon L.A., when it was best, if at all possible, to stay put, at least until dinnertime. Bolster didn't understand this incessant need to yoga-shop. It was like wanting to eat at every restaurant in the food court: you filled up, but it was temporary and unnourishing, and then soon enough you were back for more. Find a practice and commit, he thought. Make adjustments when necessary. Don't be restless. But that wasn't Suzie Hahn's way. Like a teen-ager who loved to shop, she lived perpetually in the yoga mall, God bless her.

Suzie's food arrived.

Bolster saw an opening.

"So, Chelsea Shell," he said.

"Oh, right," Suzie said. "Well, I don't like to gossip."

"Of course not."

"But the first thing you should know," she said, as she stuffed an enormous quantity of field greens into her mouth, "is that Chelsea's a man-eater."

"Really?"

"Oh, yeah. Great yoga teacher, but she just ruins guys. Literally drives them crazy."

"How so?"

"I'm not sure. Just what I hear. Don't have a lot of experience in that arena myself."

"I'm sure you have your moments, Suzie."

Suzie gave a little hair flip.

"Thank you, thank you, but I'm not really the type to play games. Besides, I'm too busy for a relationship."

It was true, Bolster thought. He'd known Suzie on and off for the better part of a decade, and he'd never seen her when she wasn't flying solo.

"I only hear rumors, of course," she said.

"Of course."

"But I think she was sleeping with Ajoy. At least at some point. She may even have been the reason he got divorced."

"I didn't know he'd gotten divorced."

"Oh, yeah, about three years ago. It was all anyone was talking about for a while."

"Guess I didn't pay attention."

"Huge scandal, lots of money involved, and they put it all on Chelsea's back. They broke up, and I heard it was ugly. He didn't dare fire her because I think she had something on him."

"Like what?"

"I'm not sure. But for someone to have that much power over Ajoy Chaterjee, that's huge. The guy didn't let people control him."

Bolster had gotten further on one bought salad than the cops would have gotten in a month. Admittedly, it was a sixteen-dollar salad, because this was the Westside. But for once, at least, he had some coin to back up his tipsters.

"You're so helpful, Suzie," he said.

"It's my yoga," she said.

When they were done, Suzie zipped off on her scooter, in time, she hoped, to make a candlelight flow class in WeHo. As the sun dipped and the night turned vaguely brisk, Bolster walked down Abbot Kinney toward home, trying to keep his thoughts sharp.

Not able to help himself, he did a Google Images search on his phone for Chelsea Shell while he walked. There were plenty of entries. She lay there on the floor, spread-eagle, with her chin in her hands and her breasts poking out indiscreetly from her lululemon top. *Oh, great.* This was the type he always wanted but shouldn't have. Bolster knew man-eaters, and one shot of this woman left him wanting to be devoured. What did they call it in the pulps? A "twisted web of desire"? Well, he felt the first strands sticking to his skin. He had a feeling that he was descending into something slowly, taking the first tentative steps into a dark cellar, with very little to light the way.

Breathe, Bolster, he said. *Exist in the present, think, and be clear. Like you know you can.*

But it was going to be tough.

———— o ————

Bolster got back to his apartment. Slim was waiting for him in the hall.

"How long you been here?" Matt said.

"Couple of hours."

"Kind of a waste of time."

"Not really. I was meditating for most of it."

"You could have called."

"Don't have a phone."

"Right. Well, come on in and get me high."

"Roger that," Slim said.

After they vaporized and watched a couple of episodes of *Archer,* Slim lay on Bolster's couch, writing poetry in a notebook. Bolster went back to the computer.

After eight years, Bolster read, Ajoy had pulled himself up to a point where he was working as a copyboy at a Kolkata newspaper, still rising at five a.m. every day to practice his yoga, and living in a mostly dry room with two other newspaper employees. One morning, as he stretched in the park, Sri Charan appeared before him, as though walking out of the mist. Ajoy saw him, walked over, and punched his guru in the face.

"You son of a whore!" he said.

"I deserved that," said Sri Charan.

"You abandoned me!"

"I did."

"Why?"

"It was part of your training. A true yogi must know all of life, both high and low."

Ajoy punched his guru in the face again.

Sri Charan laughed.

"I deserved that as well. Come, let's get you cleaned up."

So Ajoy returned to the warm embrace of his master, who didn't seem to have aged at all. He could have been anywhere between forty and eighty years old; Ajoy simply couldn't tell. Regardless, the food was better with Sri Charan, and Ajoy was ready for some relatively easy living.

They returned home to work in private beneath the great tree of Howrah. Sri Charan taught Ajoy the healing principles of ayurveda. They did advanced *pranayama* techniques. Ajoy learned to suppress the breath for thirty seconds. Then for sixty seconds. Then for longer. To be a true yogi, Sri Charan said, is to know death early. That way, you won't fear its inevitable coming, and then you'll know true freedom.

Soon, they began to develop the sequence that would someday make Ajoy famous in the West. Sri Charan knew that yoga's future lay in America. India had other work to do, but America still had a kind of open optimism and a weirdly obsessive work ethic. There, yoga could grow and thrive and blossom. Ajoy was the one, Sri Charan decided, who would bring its teachings over. This was his mission, his quest, and his destiny, in whatever form it took.

Fuck, Bolster thought. *I'm tired. Enough for tonight.* And he closed the laptop.

He'd been at it for hours. Behind him, Slim was snoring on the couch. Sometimes Bolster would come home and Slim would be snoring on the couch. There'd be days when Slim wouldn't leave the couch at all, and then he'd disappear for weeks at a time. We all have our dramas to live.

There was a knock at the door. Kind of late for company, but in Bolster's world, company could arrive at any time. Maybe Slim had texted in an order for pizza before he nodded off. Pizza sounded good right now, actually.

The knock came again.

"Coming," Bolster said.

He got up, walked over, and opened it.

That's when someone hit him in the face with a guitar.

EPISODE 2

FIVE

— o —

BOLSTER TURNED HIS HEAD SO THE GUITAR NAILED HIM ON the left side instead of straight on. He heard a cracking sound and hoped it wasn't his skull. The guitar had been swung by its neck and landed with force, like a bat striking a softball. Fortunately, the strings were facing away. At that close a distance, and with that much power, the strings could have sliced out Bolster's eyeball. Instead, his left orbital bone started to swell; he could feel it filling with fluid. His nasal cartilage hummed like a tuning fork, and his chin tingled nastily. Bolster staggered backward, catching the doorknob for support. Blood ran down his eye and into his mouth. He couldn't quite tell where it was coming from. The guitar dropped, hitting the ground with a crash. Bolster saw a pair of fashion jeans running down the outside walkway toward the stairs.

Dizziness overcame him for a second, though he didn't completely fall. All those years of doing tree pose over and over had really helped his balance in extreme circumstances, and this certainly qualified as extreme. Still holding on to the knob for support, as if it were the only piece of driftwood in the ocean, he dropped to a squat—another pose that he'd do in his sleep if it were possible.

Breathe, Bolster, he thought. *And then stand up.*

He counted to himself, trying to observe the pain, acknowledge it, and then let it go. But it's hard to practice nonattachment when you've just been hit in the face with an acoustic guitar. *I am breathing in five; I am breathing out five*, Bolster thought. He wanted to hurry but knew that if he stood too fast, he'd fall back down and then risk really severe injury. He was bad enough already. When he reached zero, he stood, steadied himself, felt surprisingly OK, and bolted out the open door toward the stairwell.

He got to the stairs in time to see a car pulling out of the parking lot, not as fast as it needed to. That's because it was a Prius—great for a casual run to Trader Joe's or to save on gas when you're stuck on the 405, not so great for fleeing the scene of an alleged assault. Bolster's legs felt strong under him as he launched himself down the outside stairs. He ran after it but couldn't stop it from leaving the complex.

"Hey, asshole!" he shouted. "Why'd you do that?"

No answer was forthcoming, though. Then the car was gone. Even a Toyota Prius could escape with enough of a head start, and Bolster was in no condition for endurance running. The car had been royal blue, he'd seen that much, but he hadn't been able to make out the rear plate. It was midnight, and he had blood dripping from his eyelashes.

A blue Prius in Los Angeles, Bolster thought. *That really narrows it down*. Maybe the cops could bring in Larry David for questioning.

He got out his cell and called Martinez, who'd been on his speed dial since lunchtime. Martinez answered on the third ring, sounding slurry. Bolster could almost smell the cheap whiskey through the phone.

"Whazamatter, Bolster," Martinez said.

"Someone just came to my house and hit me in the face with a guitar."

"Ouch."

"Damn right, ouch."

"Didya see him?"

"Only his jeans."

"His jeans?"

"He hit me kinda quick."

"Right."

"He drove away in a Prius, but I didn't get the plate."

"Why the fuck don't people drive real cars anymore?"

"I don't know."

"All right," Martinez said.

There was a little pause.

"I'm really drunk right now, Bolster."

"I can tell."

"Do you need the cops tonight?"

"No."

"I'll call you in the morning, OK?"

"Yeah, that's fine."

"Put some ice on it or go to the hospital or something."

"Very helpful, Martinez."

Martinez didn't hang up, but he didn't talk anymore, either. Bolster guessed he'd fallen asleep. He was tempted to keep the phone on just to run up Martinez's minutes, but he decided against it; he disconnected and went back upstairs.

Bolster's apartment door was still open. The guitar lay across the entry, nearly cracked in half. Matt bent down. The side that had hit him bore little specks of his blood. It had folded inward—obviously some sort of cheap plywood or balsa backing, half a step better than industrial-grade paper. Whoever had come for him hadn't bothered to bust out the best china. Bolster didn't warrant that. Yet.

Standing up, Bolster saw that someone had taped a note to his doorway, written in fussy cursive letters on a torn-out piece of legal-pad paper. *Sloppy work*, Bolster thought. *You should have typed and laser-printed it. Cops can get handwriting samples.* Of course, "can" was the key word. Even with a big celebrity murder on its hands, the LAPD didn't usually spend a lot of time matching curlicues. This wasn't *Criminal Minds*.

"Dear Mat," the note read. Bolster winced at the misspelling of his name and wasn't sure if it had been deliberate or not. "If you're thinking about asking any more questions about Ajoy Yoga, then think again. Yoga is more mysterious than you might imagine, and there's more to Ajoy than just some sequence of poses. By dying that way, Ajoy may have just been saving your life, and mine. Keep out of our business. We don't want to hurt you again, but we will. Remember that the journey to truth begins in ignorance." It was signed: "Namaste, a friend."

Some friend, Bolster thought.

And what a weird note. What did it mean by "dying that way"? Had Ajoy *chosen* the manner of his own death? How? Why? The whole thing seemed very unlikely. Even if it were so, why would he have picked such a grisly death? Why were yoga people all so fucked up?

True yogis were supposed to practice *ahimsa*, the karmic principle of nonviolence. Yes, in the *Baghavad Gita*, Arjuna is forced to take his people to war at the exact moment of his enlightenment, but those were, to say the least, unusual circumstances. Sometimes you have to fight. But murder's never OK. And neither is hitting someone in the face with a guitar, unprovoked.

What a punk, Bolster thought. He clenched his fists. *I've got your nonviolence right here, pal.*

Bolster observed his anger, cradling it in his metaphorical hands like a kitten, as Thich Naht Hanh teaches. It washed over him. He felt it fully, and then he let it go.

Calmer now, Bolster went into his kitchen, got a rag, picked up the shattered guitar with it, and brought the guitar inside. Then he went into the bathroom to examine the damage. There was just a small cut over the eye, not too deep, and a little redness on the cheekbone. He felt slightly queasy, like he might have a minor concussion. It wouldn't be the first time.

No headstands for me this week, he thought.

He looked up from the sink, where he'd been splashing water. A guy was standing at the bathroom door. Bolster jumped a little. But it was just Slim, who'd been sleeping on the couch the whole time.

"What happened to you?" Slim asked.

"Let's get a pizza," Bolster said.

Bolster woke at ten, feeling crappy. His head was sore inside and out, and his gut churned from his two a.m. bullshit session with Slim. Too many of his days started in a fog. He thought about giving up the weed, but that would mean giving up the weed. Some attachments were hard to break.

He had to teach in an hour. There was no room for slack this morning, because the studio was at least half an hour away, worse if there was traffic, and there was always traffic. Pushing away the sheets, Bolster saw that he was naked. Sometimes he flopped that way. He pulled a pair of stretchy shorts off the pile, as well as a turquoise muscle shirt that had an old-school Las Vegas tourism logo embossed in the middle. At the end of his classes, all of his students had gotten their workouts and could claim their peace of mind, so who cared what the teacher wore? Besides, these clothes were cheap, and Bolster loved wearing cheap clothes.

The living room bore signs of a dude debacle. Slim had mysteriously vanished with the dawn, like Batman, but hadn't bothered cleaning. Smashed guitar aside, there were empty pizza boxes, beer bottles, and stubby roaches on the coffee table. The TV was paused on a screenshot of Kenny Powers giving someone the finger. *A good time was had by all*, Bolster thought.

Except the times weren't so good. As he put the kettle on to boil, Bolster thought some more about what had happened. He'd been on the case for fewer than twelve hours when someone had attacked him, and he'd questioned only one person so far. That meant that Casey Anderson must have talked to someone. Unless…

Suzie Hahn.

Dammit.

He dialed. She answered on the first ring. No one in the world was easier to contact than Suzie Hahn.

"Hi, Matt!" she said. "How's it going?"

"Suzie," he said, "did you tell anyone that we talked?"

"Of course!" she said. "I put it on my blog as soon as I could."

"Really," he said.

Matt flipped open his laptop and went to Suzie's site. The lead post, which had gone up at 8:49 the night before, was titled, "Ace Yoga Teacher PI Matt Bolster Is on the Case!"

"Everyone's favorite detective turned yoga teacher, Matt Bolster, has contracted with the LAPD to solve the murder of Ajoy Chaterjee, our sources tell us," the post began.

Bolster had already seen enough.

"Suzie," he said, "we weren't talking on the record."

"Oh my gosh!" she said. "I'm sorry. I just assumed that you needed help. I put your contact information up in case people wanted to contact you with tips."

"Did that include my address?"

"Whoops," she said.

"Yeah," said Bolster.

"I'll take it down as soon as I'm done with morning *kirtan*," she said.

"Please do."

"Oh, and Matt?"

"Yes?"

"You might want to talk to Martha Wickman. She runs the Ajoy studio in Atwater Village, and she knew Ajoy a really long time."

"Thanks for that, Suzie."

"No problem! And have a great class today! I know you'll do awesome!"

"How did you know I was teaching?"

"I know when *everyone's* teaching," she said.

Bolster wanted to stay mad at Suzie, but he never could.

There were few worse ways to make a living than by teaching yoga. Even in Southern California, with its limitless supply of insecure, body-conscious actors and aimless weirdos, Bolster had almost infinite competition. The major studios churned out hundreds of new "teachers" a month, many of whom knew next to nothing about yoga yet immediately plugged themselves into the teacher-training circuit. With every generation of trainees, the wisdom became thinner and more received, further and further away from the source. The industry played this continual game of telephone with people's souls, and the teachings got more and more distorted. Most of the people innocently signing up for class passes had no idea of the enlightenment machine into which they were grinding themselves.

Bolster got only seven people in his class, and they "donated" a total of sixty-five dollars. After paying the studio its forty-dollar rental fee, Bolster would walk out with twenty-five hot ones in his pocket. That could get him through a day in L.A.—as long as he didn't spend any of it. The crime-solving business, while certainly not consistent either, still paid better.

"What happened to your face?" asked one of his students.

"I fell while I was practicing side crow," he said. "This yoga is a dangerous business."

They laughed and nodded in understanding, or what they thought was understanding. Doing yoga had many advantages. But one of the least known, or discussed, was the fact that you could use it as an excuse to cover up just about any crap that had happened to you the night before.

Bolster put his students through a tough, almost relentless workout: lots of *vinyasa*, very little explanation, and only just enough rest to keep them from complaining. They jumped, twisted, bent forward and back, and were sweating pretty good by the time it was all over. Sometimes Bolster rolled it out that way, and today he was feeling pretty aggressive, to the point that he practiced along with most of the class. He had some mental knots to work through.

There was no music. Occasionally Bolster played some mellow tunes during wind-down and *savasana*, but most of the time it seemed like too much trouble. Teachers who bragged about their awesome yoga mixes and who urged students to "rock their *asana*" were often covering for a lack of training, he thought. Bolster liked music, of course, and he liked yoga, but he didn't necessarily think they had to go together. Any such claims were just trendy garbage. Music was more a distraction than an enhancement to him.

Maybe that's why he had only seven students in his class.

Afterward, Bolster got into his ride, a 1998 Nissan Sentra that had once been bone-white but now was a sort of off-gray. He called his car Whitey anyway, out of ironic affection. Crappy old midsize cars needed love, too, and, what the hell, he'd paid it off years ago. The fabric seats were very Akron Greyhound terminal in their color and design and bore their share of snags and burns. Whitey had a steering wheel so loose that Bolster sometimes feared it would twist off in his hands. The car had suffered some minor electrical meltdowns; its driver's-side window switch hadn't worked for a while. Bolster had covered it with electrical tape to remind himself not to press down. The window wouldn't rise again on its own.

Someday, when he had $275 to spare, he might return Whitey to full health. Maybe if he solved Ajoy's murder. That's what it came to in this town. Fifty grand didn't mean Bolster could buy a house, or take a vacation, or do anything of importance, but at least he could get Whitey's window fixed.

He put on a clean T-shirt, pulled a pair of cargo pants over his stanky yoga shorts, and daubed his wet pits with a little Old Spice that he kept in the glove box. The phone rang. It was Martinez.

"How's your head?" he asked.

"Sore," said Bolster.

"You got anything?"

"There are a couple of leads."

"And?"

"And I'm getting to them. I had to teach this morning."

"We're not paying you to teach yoga."

"It's an avocation," Bolster said. "What's your story?"

"Not a fucking thing," said Martinez. "Ajoy's autopsy is tomorrow morning. County morgue."

"'Yah Mo B There.'" Bolster said. "Wouldn't miss it. That guy had muscles where muscles shouldn't be."

"All right."

"Oh, hey, Martinez?"

"What?"

"If you're asking around today, try to find out who hit me in the fucking face."

"I'll get right on that, sport," Martinez said.

Bolster started the car. It made a sound like a rheumatic war veteran, but at least it sparked. He had a woman to see in Atwater. This time of day, that was about a forty-five-minute trip. He hoped he had enough gas to get there. He hoped Whitey wouldn't let him down.

But Whitey sometimes did.

SIX

○

THE CAR HAD A TAPE DECK. BOLSTER'S LAST REMAINING cassette was *Exile on Main St.*, but you can only listen to an album so many times, even one as great as that. He'd bought a cheap cassette adapter at Radio Shack so he could stream off his phone. That was how, on the drive over to Atwater, he found himself listening to an Audible file of *I Became Yoga*, Ajoy Chaterjee's two-volume autobiography. Bolster found it eerie to be listening to Ajoy's words. Well, technically they weren't his words, since there'd been a ghostwriter. But it was still Ajoy on his car stereo nonetheless, as though he were speaking from beyond the grave.

Bolster skipped Ajoy's boyhood creation myth, since that was all still fresh in his mind, and went straight to the '70s. Ajoy was saying:

"Sri Charan told me, 'Ajoy, the West is weak in yoga. You must become yoga. You must embody it. You need to teach them what it means. But we have to present it in a form that they understand. Americans don't understand nonattachment. They are attached to everything—to their dogs, to their cars, to their televisions, to their hamburgers. They are fat and dumb and weak, like moronic children afraid to lose their favorite toys.' I thought that he was being perhaps a little harsh, but he was an older man by that point and could get somewhat grouchy. 'What do you suggest?'

I asked. And Sri Charan said, 'The only way to get Americans to calm down is to make them exercise.'"

Well, there you have it, Bolster thought. The modern yoga craze, hatched by a couple of provincial Bengali lunatics in an arboretum. On the recording, Ajoy continued his now post-humous narrative. In that park, under the banyan tree, he and Sri Charan developed Ajoy's sequence, which Madonna would one day lionize in a lesser-known dance-club B-side called "The Sequence." It was twenty-eight poses and included variations for different levels of comfort and ability. It would, in Ajoy's ghostwriter's words, "help cure humankind of all its maladies, physical, emotional, and spiritual. It would leave no body part untouched, no gland uninfluenced, no chakra unaligned. We had found the key to health and happiness."

In 1974, Ajoy Chaterjee traveled to the United States for the first time. He had a hundred dollars and the address of Sri Charan's great-nephew, who was a chemical engineering student at UCLA, in his pocket. Then Ajoy was in L.A., where every man's shirt seemed to be open one button too many. It was an era of hairy chests.

Ajoy moved into the nephew's studio apartment, sometimes sleeping in the bathtub if the nephew ever invited a friend to spend the night. He had nothing but his mission, and took it to various parks in Westwood and Beverly Hills, sometimes hitch-hiking down to Venice Beach, which was much scruffier in those days. He propped up a piece of cardboard with the words "YOGA LESSONS" scrawled in black marker on it, and began doing poses there on the grass. Most of his early clients were homeless. Everyone else pretty much ignored him for months.

Almost no one was doing yoga in the '70s. Crazy gurus could get tens of thousands to believe that they would levitate the Astrodome, and plenty of people were doing Transcendental Meditation. But in those days, *hatha*, or physical, yoga was as remote a concept as spinning class. There had been previous crazes, but it was currently dormant. As Ajoy said in his book, "I was having difficulty persuading people in the salutary benefits of standing on your head in public. Perhaps if I had done it while wearing a nice leisure suit, I would have attracted a wealthier clientele."

Bolster found himself actually liking this version of Ajoy. The man had humor. He understood the tender mix of naive optimism, mordancy, and herdlike consumer behavior that comprises the American mind. But cashing in takes time.

One afternoon, Ajoy had put up his shingle in Westwood and was encountering the usual indifference. A chubby young coed approached with interest in her eyes. Ajoy stood on a lawn on one leg, hands in *namaskar*, his eyes staring peacefully ahead. His other leg was twisted at the hip and folded behind his neck. He wore a blue headband and a spandex American-flag loincloth.

"Hello," the coed said.

"May I help you?" asked Ajoy.

"I'd like some yoga lessons," she said.

"She would become my first and best student," Ajoy said later in his autobiography.

Her name was Martha Wickman.

———————— o ————————

Ajoy had many keys to business success. But a major one seemed to be an almost psychic inclination toward real-estate bargains. He never, ever owned, and always leased retail space in locations where the price never really seemed to go up. "I have no interest in being trendy," he said once to *Time* magazine. "The trends will come to *me*." True to form, Ajoy Yoga Atwater was two rooms in a strip mall between a gas station and an I-5 overpass. Its immediate neighbors were a payday loan joint and a postal-supplies store.

Still, when Bolster pulled up in Whitey at a quarter of two, there was a line of people and mats spilling into the parking lot. In most of the country, two p.m. was the time of day when yoga-studio owners went home, juiced some wheatgrass, and perused bankruptcy attorney websites. Not Los Angeles. You could fill a yoga studio any time of day. No one worked regular hours in this town. People just ate lunch and waited for their agents to call.

Bolster got in line like everyone else. He didn't think that a crowd of people whose de facto cult leader had just been murdered would take well to a guy pushing past them saying, "Excuse me, I'm a private investigator." Usually, he tried to do his business on the down-low.

After about five minutes, he reached the desk, operated by a young woman with blank eyes and perfect skin, clearly identifying her as a fervent practitioner of The Sequence. *You're gonna die, too, someday*, Bolster wanted to say to these yoga zombies. But he didn't, because that was rarely what people wanted to hear.

"Can I help you?" the yoga zombie asked.

"I'm looking for Martha Wickman," he said.

"Drop-in?"

"Um, yeah, I guess I'm dropping in."

"OK, that's twenty dollars."

"Twenty dollars to talk to Martha?"

"No, Martha is teaching at two. That's why there are so many people."

"Oh."

"She was the first one to learn The Sequence."

"So I've heard. But listen, I just want to talk with her."

"You can talk to her after class."

"But…"

"Do you want to take it?"

Fuck no, Bolster thought. Ajoy Yoga was brutal. He'd challenged himself once and practiced The Sequence every day for a week. Not only had he been impossibly sore when it was over, but his mind and body had been so drained that he'd spent one Sunday drooling on himself while watching an *Antiques Roadshow* marathon. It wasn't his yoga. But now he had an assignment.

"Sure," he said, and handed over his debit card, thinking, *Twenty bucks to make fifty grand. Not so bad.*

"Do you have a towel?" the zombie asked.

Bolster had his mat bag, which always contained a couple of clean hand towels and a yoga strap. Douglas Adams was right. You never leave home without a towel. Particularly not when your professional obligations include sweating profusely.

Bolster went into the studio, which could fit maybe fifty people before the fire marshal would shut it down. The room was stuffy, windowless, and dark, the only dim light coming from a creepy vintage chandelier—a fetish of Ajoy's, whose decorative taste could be described as Buddhist monk meets Liberace—and a couple of long-burning candles at the front of the room, where students and teachers had set up an impromptu memorial for their slain leader. Ajoy's portrait sat atop some sort of stool or steps, which had been covered in velvet and festooned with flower petals and little pieces of candy. Ajoy had loved candy, and he'd eaten it all the time, carrying it in a leather pouch attached to his stretchy shorts. He didn't allow his students to share, because they hadn't yet completed his cleansing program. "When you develop your own sequence, then you can have candy," he was fond of saying.

This wasn't "hot yoga." They didn't jack it up to 105 like Bikram did. But it wasn't cold, either. The air smelled dank, like a cheese wheel gone to mold. It hit Bolster like a stink bomb in a movie theater. The room had been divided into "Sequence Squares" in thin blue masking tape, with just enough space for a mat and a body. Almost all of them were already full, so Bolster had to take one toward the middle back, just to the left of a padded support column.

After he situated himself, he took in the scene. People sat on their mats looking scared, like paratroopers about to jump behind enemy lines. They were all half-naked. Some gazed at themselves in one of the half dozen body mirrors placed around the room at precise intervals. One guy in the front corner was wearing nothing but a maroon-colored diaper and matching headband; he meditated showily, muscles tensed and looking full of purpose. There was a quiet, invisible intensity about, a feeling of energy being stored up, ready to explode. You couldn't hear anything but raspy, rhythmic breathing. Bolster sensed that he'd accidentally stumbled into a meaningful experience, his least favorite kind. Meaning leads to attachment, and attachment leads to suffering. These people, who practiced Ajoy Yoga nearly every day of their lives, suffered more than most. A collective madness brewed. Bolster just hoped he could make it out intact.

An older woman appeared at the front of the room. She had legs like stumps and a sharp jawline that indicated a unique dedication to a singular purpose. Her eyes were as clear as the water in an undiscovered Mexican cenote. She wore a plain white T-shirt and a pair of decidedly untrendy workout shorts. Bolster was impressed by Martha Wickman immediately. In a world of cookie-cutter, Barbie doll yoga teachers, she stood nearly alone, more Large Marge than lululemon ambassador. This woman knew what she was doing. Unfortunately, what she was doing would be considered torture in many civilized realms. Bolster could do nothing to prepare himself.

"The father of us all is dead," Martha Wickman said.

Way to cut to the core, lady, Bolster thought.

"There's nothing any of us can do to change that fact. Ajoy didn't want to die any more than the rest of us. But I think we all know what he would want us to do now, right?"

Martha Wickman cupped a hand to her ear.

"*The Sequence!*" shouted everyone in unison.

Bolster hated it when Ajoy people did that. It made them sound like a cult, at least a borderline one.

"That's right," said Martha. "Practice is the only thing that can truly help us get through our grief. So I don't think we should sit around and tell weepy stories about how much we loved Ajoy. There'll be plenty of time for that crap. I'd rather get started, wouldn't you?"

"*Yes!*" the class chanted.

She turned her eyes to the sky.

"I dedicate this practice to you, Ajoy Chaterjee," she said. "My guru and my friend."

For the next hour and a half, Bolster bent brutally. But he was obviously a junior member of the corps. Martha kept giving him adjustments, wrenching him into twists that he hated, propping up joints that just wanted to hang loose. At one point, while he was in an impossibly long bow pose, she lifted up his shoulders with ferocious strength and power, as if she were trying to move a desk across the room. Bolster knew that he'd have trouble lifting a pen tomorrow. His face pounded where the guitar had struck. He hated it when teachers touched him.

Around him, the other students went through their Sequences with religious purpose. They gazed with frightening intent, wringing out their *samskara* like it really mattered. Bolster knew it didn't—that happiness and hard work didn't always go together—but he let it go. If people had to put themselves through a sausage grinder to get through the day, he shouldn't judge. The room felt sluggish and sour.

By the time they hit *savasana*, a few students were openly sobbing, while others moaned quietly. Bolster had been to some weird memorial services in his time, but this was close to a topper. He endured, though, because he had work to do.

"Now, you all must pretend to die," said Martha Wickman. "Because that's all that yoga is. Rehearsal for death. And no one rehearsed harder than our late guru."

Bolster understood this but thought it was maybe a little much. He usually referred to *savasana*, in his classes, as "the golden nap." That was an easier sell than "rehearsal for death." But clearly Martha Wickman didn't go in for the easy sell. He just hoped she was a little less intense off the mat. Either way, his glutes were already sore.

SEVEN

○

AFTER CLASS, BOLSTER'S LEGS FELT RUBBERY AND HIS MIND didn't feel much better. He needed to smoke a joint and drink a sixteen-ounce Coke Zero. That'd spark the brain.

He went up to Martha Wickman.

"Hi," he said. "I'm—"

"I know who you are, Matt Bolster," she said.

"How?" he said. "We never met before."

"I read Suzie Hahn's blog."

"You do?"

"Everyone does," Martha said.

"Oh."

"I figured you'd show up. I had special adjustments ready. You deserve a little pain."

"I don't think I do."

"Naw, I'm just kidding," she said, slapping him on the back.

"Glad to hear it."

"Actually, I appreciate you caring enough to ask the tough questions."

"But I *don't* care," Bolster said. "I'm just doing this to get paid."

"I appreciate the honesty, too," she said.

Bolster wasn't being totally honest. He did care, at least a little. Ajoy was the public face of yoga to a lot of people. Obviously, something had gone malignant in the system. Yoga was too important for him to allow it to fester. Practicing yoga made so many people happy so much of the time. But, like most great powers, it could also be used for evil.

"Regardless," Bolster said, "I'd like to talk to you."

"We can talk now," Martha said. "Are you hungry?"

Bolster was, indeed, really, really hungry. He'd taught a class and had been through another brutal one. To compensate, he'd eaten a banana for breakfast and then a handful of almonds that he'd found in Whitey's glove compartment. God knows how old those had been.

"Yes," he said.

"Good," she said. "Then you can take me to In-N-Out Burger."

Bolster was surprised, though not unpleasantly so, to hear those words coming from a yoga master. He tried to eat healthfully most of the time. But In-N-Out Burger was a sacred temple.

"Anytime," he said.

They sat by the window of the In-N-Out in Glendale, just south of the Americana mall. The clientele was a mix: fat guys and their sons wearing Dodgers shirts, Chinese families, black teenagers, some hipster types slumming it, and, because of the location, more than a few Armenian thugs. In other words, America, which was one of the reasons Bolster liked coming here. It was one of the few places left where you could really bear witness to the gathering of the tribes.

Bolster ordered off the burger joint's "secret menu," which was about as secret as the address of city hall, but he liked the idea of speaking in food code. So he got a Double-Double, animal style, but without the spread and the onions. Essentially, that was a cheeseburger with mustard cooked into the patty. Also, he got his fries well done, which made them like matchstick potatoes, and a chocolate shake. Martha sat across from him with two single burgers, protein style, which meant wrapped in lettuce leaves instead of a bun. This really was the greatest place.

Martha told her story.

"I went up to Ajoy in the park that day in 1974 and asked him to teach me yoga," Martha was saying. "He untangled from his position and immediately, right there in the park, put me through the Sequence. It was the toughest hour and a half of my life up to that point, but I made my way through. If I had trouble with a pose, he laughed gently and showed me something easier. That's what Ajoy lost in the later years: that gentle laughter. He really was a sweet soul under all that bluster."

"Were you in love with him?" Bolster asked, finding himself surprised to throw out such a blunt question. But Martha didn't seem to care.

"Not romantically," she said. "Ajoy could be a rude bastard. The only time he grabbed my ass during practice, like, two years in, I twisted his balls and said, 'You do that again, and I'll make you a eunuch.' He thought that was great. 'Maybe you can put my balls on your mantle, like a trophy.' 'Well,' I said, 'it *would* scare away the burglars.'"

"Good one," said Bolster.

"But, I mean, I did *love* him, of course," she said. "He was my guru, my mentor, and my friend. He absolutely opened the secrets of the universe to me. I see clearly and walk the earth with confidence today because of him, no doubt."

"That doesn't sound like cult-leader behavior."

"Ajoy wasn't a cult leader," Martha said. "He was an actor, yes, and a strong businessman. But all he really wanted to do was teach yoga. It's all these students who turned it into a cult."

"How do you mean?"

"They started bringing him flowers, they baked him cakes, they wrote songs about him. Ajoy accepted the gifts because he didn't want to be rude, but he hated that shit, mostly. I saw it happen. For years, we just had that little studio on San Vicente, mostly Ajoy and me teaching, and then every couple of years he'd certify a few people so we could have substitutes and take vacations. We'd get the occasional rich producer type. Mostly, though, it was regular people doing their practice and then drinking tea and laughing."

"Sounds pretty nice," Bolster said.

"It was," she said. "But then it started to turn. People in this town are so fragile, they'll latch on to anything and make it into a cult. The yoga lays traps for them."

"It does," Bolster said.

"Ajoy's Sequence started getting attention, and these rich clients would take him away on private weekends and pay him tens of thousands of dollars. He made them feel good, because that's what he did, but in return, they started pumping his ego. And once someone believes he's a master, he loses all mastery."

"Indeed," said Bolster.

"So with money came business, and with business came marketing, and with marketing came the sheep. Suddenly, Ajoy had groupies. He took it all with good humor, but the change in the culture was remarkable. Studios started to spread, people started forming alliances, and it got a little out of control. I just kept teaching the Sequence like I always had, but there were variations, and music, and a clothing line, and the shit multiplied. Ajoy was always more of a money guy than a sex guy anyway. He could get laid if he wanted to, with that body, but he was really poor for much of his adult life. So when the money started coming in, that's when it got weird."

"Yeah," Bolster said, sucking on a french fry. "You never hear a lot of the sex rumors about Ajoy like you do about the other teachers."

"He was pretty happily married there, for a lot of years, until…"

"Until what?" Bolster said.

"Until Chelsea Shell came to town."

"What happened then?"

"Ajoy stopped thinking around that woman. No one had ever made him lose control like that, and this was a man who spent many intimate hours in close physical contact with some of the hottest starlets in the world. But when she was in the room, he'd sit in the corner, blushing like a teenager. He did anything she asked, and she rose through the ranks of senior teachers *fast*."

"Were they fucking?"

"Probably. Maybe. Or maybe not. I don't know. I mean, they certainly weren't *exclusive*. But Chelsea had him, and she knew it."

"Dammit," Matt said.

"What?"

"I'm gonna have to go talk to this Chelsea Shell, aren't I?"

"Probably."

"All right." He sighed. "Where can I find her?"

"She works at a studio in West Hollywood above a juice place."

"That really narrows it down."

Martha scribbled the address on the back of an In-N-Out napkin.

"She's teaching at six. You can probably still make it."

"All right," Matt said.

"Well," Martha said.

"Well," said Bolster.

"Thanks for the burgers, Matt."

"My pleasure," he said. "By the way, I don't think you did it."

"Honey," Martha said, "if I didn't kill Ajoy thirty years ago, I certainly wasn't going to do it now."

Bolster stood up to leave. As he walked away, Martha said, "You be good, now, private dick." And then she smacked Bolster on the ass.

Well, that was a weird thing to do, Bolster thought.

But even weirder was the fact that he'd liked it.

EIGHT

―――――――― o ――――――――

B OLSTER DROVE, AT RUSH HOUR, THROUGH THE MOST crowded urban roads in North America. He needed to cover fewer than eight miles yet worried that an hour and a half wouldn't be nearly enough time. It would have been an unpleasant trip even in the most hermetically sealed luxury car, but with his ancient, Japanese tin bucket, he might as well have been wandering the streets naked. He absorbed every sound and smell, as though the car's exterior and interior had somehow been magically reversed. And it didn't matter how many podcasts he listened to. He was still bored.

Even though Bolster didn't live on the Eastside, these streets still seemed familiar to him. Because of the way he'd spent his youth, he felt that way about most of the city. Though the storefronts had shifted somewhat over the years, the general makeup hadn't changed much. Lower Santa Monica, from Silver Lake through Mid-City, was a loving Michoacán-meets-Seoul mashup of Central American restaurants, low-rent pot shops, *eloteros* and *paleteros* pushing their carts, community-college students spilling out by the hundreds, sooty repair shops, and Korean barbecue joints that couldn't afford the rent on Wilshire. The overpriced gas stations began to appear a few blocks before the 101 on-ramps, alongside fast-food joints and some of the dingiest rental housing this side of the Tijuana slums. Alongside Bolster drove the most wretched collection of third-rate automotive conveyances imaginable: cars on their third or fourth owner, cars missing windows, bumpers, headlights, and, in one extreme case, a rear driver's-side door. These were thousand-dollar cars. They were hundred-dollar cars. By comparison, Bolster felt like he drove in shameless luxury. Then again, these cars ran (most of them, anyway), they got their people around (most of the time), and they weren't getting stolen. If they had been stolen, it had happened a long time ago, and they'd never found their way home.

Then he went past the world's largest batting cage, and suddenly the landscape shifted. Restaurants got more upscale, and so did the head shops. There were art galleries and furniture stores, and signs of valet life. Gourmet-tea boutiques abutted specialty-eyewear stores. Suddenly, Whitey looked very low-rent. The street got quieter, too. People were in their cars listening to NPR, not booming the bass. *Change is the only constant*, Bolster thought. *We're on this earth to observe the process of change, to see reality in its true nature, as it unfolds, without judgment.* Fancy people, poor people, nice cars, and junkers: all one under the ever-watchful eye of pure awareness. At least, that was the idea.

At last, Bolster arrived at YogaLife™, an "Ajoy-inspired" studio not all that far away from where Ajoy had been murdered. But culturally, it was another country. Whereas Ajoy's flagship studio had kept things pretty no-frills and low-key, YogaLife was appealing to a much more upmarket crowd. It had valet parking, good for up to four hours with validation; full-service men's and women's locker rooms with individual shower stalls; and a sizable boutique selling yoga clothes, DVDs, books, CDs, hemp sandals, natural bath salts, healing crystals, tapestries with inspirational quotes sewn into them, candles, protein bars, fourteen different varieties of yoga mats, and photos of the Dalai Lama. YogaLife wasn't just selling yoga, it was selling the "yoga lifestyle," and in Bolster's experience, those often meant two very different things.

He approached the reception area, which wouldn't have been out of place at a Condé Nast magazine office.

"Hi," he said.

"Hi," said the pretty, blasé yoga creature behind the desk. "Are you here for candlelight flow?"

Oh, sweet Krishna, Bolster thought to himself. *Not candlelight flow. Anything but that.* Candlelight flow, in his experience, meant ladies sharing their feelings and opening their hearts to the sky. He had no interest in either.

"Is Chelsea teaching it?" he said.

"She is," said the desk girl.

"Then sure," he said.

"That'll be eighteen dollars."

Bolster handed his money over reluctantly. He'd already spent one and a half times as much money on yoga today as he'd earned teaching. This simply wasn't a sustainable lifestyle unless there were two or more yoga murders for him to solve every year. Bolster supposed anything was possible.

In exchange for his pound of flesh, Bolster got a locker key and a complimentary glass of cucumber-infused water. That tasted pretty refreshing. He turned down the offer to rent a towel for a dollar, since he still had a clean one in his mat bag.

Inside the studio, Bolster could see that he was in for a twenty-five-person class, and that he was the only heterosexual man in the room, not that he minded. You get used to that in yoga-land. He realized that, including the one he'd taught, this would be his third yoga class since breakfast. Hopefully it would be his last. He also hoped they didn't do a lot of serious twisting. He had about half a pound of cheeseburger, plus a milk shake, sloshing around in his belly. It was a recipe for toxic disaster.

The room was dimly lit, with candles arranged all around. *Kirtan* music played softly—American-recorded arrangements of ancient Sanskrit chants. No matter how superficially beautiful, Bolster always thought *kirtan* sounded wrong in these contexts, like guitar in church. Yet every day millions of Americans listened to it, praying to a god they didn't know in a language they could never begin to understand.

As the students entered, they approached the "teacher's mat," which had already been set up at the front of the room, with little offerings. Some brought flowers, others brought bits of candy or individually wrapped chocolates. Another had the temerity to drop off a jewel-case CD labeled "Yoga Teaching Demo Reel."

At the exact moment when class was supposed to start, Chelsea Shell appeared, dirty-blonde hair done up in a ponytail. She wore a low-cut flowery top that accentuated her breasts, sure, but really showed off her strong shoulders and sinewy arm muscles, which practically screamed flexibility and excellence. Her eyes shined like jewels, and her legs moved like those of a jungle animal in full stride, even though she couldn't have been much taller than five foot five. She was magnificent to behold, and behind her trailed some sort of unknown bewitchery. Who knew from whence she drew her power? Bolster was impressed.

"Sorry I'm late, guys," she said. "But I got a phone call—you know, the kind of call you don't really want to get but that you have to take anyway because it's just so *interesting*?"

Oh, I do, I do, Bolster thought sardonically. He hated it when yoga teachers talked about their personal lives, as though their problems were somehow more important than everyone else's because they did "spiritual" work. He was already biased against this Chelsea Shell.

"Well, that's all over now, and we're here together, so I have an idea: let's all start on our backs so we can tune in to the evening together. We're going to breathe together now, and when you breathe, I want you to feel the *vibrations* of your breath. The in vibrations and the out vibrations. It's important to feel all the vibrations, because that's what we really are, and nothing more."

Bolster did as she commanded. After all, he was composed only of vibrations, like everyone else. Besides, he wanted to be on his back for a little while. It had been a hell of a couple of days, and he needed the break, and the breath. Maybe he should revise his opinion of Chelsea Shell.

"Put your right hand three inches below your navel," Chelsea Shell was saying, "and breathe rhythmically in and out."

Chelsea's voice was incredibly soothing—warm, buttery, and soft. A lotion bath. Bolster found himself drawn toward her instructions, and beyond. Only three more inches before his right hand was where he *really* wanted it to be. What was wrong with him? He never got horny in yoga class, particularly not while listening to Jai Uttal. But Chelsea Shell had some sort of strange power. Never before had he gone from loathing to lust for a person in such a short window, though maybe, he thought, loathing and lust were really just the same emotion seen from different perspectives.

His eyes were closed. He felt a pair of hands, soft and sweet-smelling but also hard and affirmative. They massaged his temples.

"As you breathe in and out, put the pressures of the day far behind you."

But Matt had a feeling that the day's pressures were only just beginning.

———————— o ————————

After class, Bolster approached Chelsea Shell. He had to wait a while because she was surrounded by gay acolytes, who were showering her with praise. This was West Hollywood, after all. Anyone with any kind of status had gay acolytes. Bolster had to admit that he felt pretty good, more relaxed than usual after yoga. He floated on a cloud of warmth.

The crowd dispersed slowly, like spilled oil being treated with chemicals, but Bolster finally had his shot. He felt odd—a middle-school kid with a crush on his foxy art teacher. He gulped.

"Excuse me, Miss Shell, I'm—"

She looked at him, eyes burning with amusement and intensity.

"I know who you are, Matt Bolster," she said.

"Oh, then you must read Suzie Hahn's blog," he joked.

"I have no idea what that is."

"Then how?"

"Because there are things *I know*."

Tread carefully, Matt, Bolster thought. And then he did the exact opposite by asking Chelsea Shell out to dinner.

"I'm not hungry, myself," he said. "I had a burger three hours ago."

"I know that, too," said Chelsea. "I can smell it on you."

"You're like a dog," Bolster said.

Chelsea Shell raised her eyebrows. She wasn't used to being called a dog.

"A very attractive, purebred dog," he added.

"That's better," she said, laughing and touching his shoulder gently. Bolster felt really good, almost gooey. That couldn't be helpful. He had questions to ask this woman.

"Let's get a smoothie downstairs," she said.

Bolster suspected that Chelsea Shell was involved with the Ajoy murder in some strange way, even if she hadn't been the specific person to flash the *Khechari* knife. She came up in every conversation and seemed to be on everyone's mind. Obviously— he could tell from her class alone—she possessed some sort of strange *siddhis*, the extraordinary yoga abilities described in the legendary sutras of Patanjali. Rarely, though, were yogis and yoginis able to overcome temptation and use those powers for good. Over a sixteen-ounce apple-carrot-ginger purée, which tasted disgusting (and cost him $9.50, for God's sake), Bolster had a chance to submit her to the kind of tough grilling that made him such an effective private investigator.

"So," he said, "tell me about yourself."

Way to come at her hard, Bolster.

"Well," she said, "I grew up in Ohio. My dad was an executive at a tire company, and my mother was a school nurse. I was a cheerleader in high school, believe it or not."

"I believe it," Bolster said.

"But I was also a total drama nerd. I started doing plays in eighth grade. My first one was *Once Upon a Mattress*."

"That was everyone's first play," Matt said.

"Oh, were you an actor, too?"

"Only because I liked the girls. They were crazy. Legitimately."

"Ha!" said Chelsea Shell. "So true. Anyway, I went to Ohio State and did the theater program there, and then I moved out to L.A., because, well, for the same reasons everyone does."

"Because they secretly hate themselves?"

"You're funny," she said. "Yes, that, but also because I wanted to break in. You can imagine how that went."

"I can."

"Not well. After five years, I had nothing to show for my time here but a few stupid ex-boyfriends, a few bad waitressing jobs, a lot of ticket stubs from the Vista Theater and the Wiltern, a minor cocaine habit, and a roommate who hated me."

"Then, let me guess: you found yoga."

"*But of course*," she said with a fake French accent, and Bolster thought he would die. "A friend took me to Ajoy's studio on San Vicente, and from the moment I started the Sequence, I knew I'd found my life's passion."

Yoga, Bolster wondered, *or Ajoy Chaterjee?*

"I felt so good when I was done," she continued, "that I just knew I had to do it again. Immediately, I bought a pass, and I started doing Ajoy's one-month challenge. But I quickly found that once a day wasn't enough for me. I started going about ten times a week."

"Maybe you were replacing your coke habit," Bolster said.

"Yeah, maybe," she said. "But yoga's a lot better for you than blow."

"Can't argue with that," he said.

"Anyway, at some point, Ajoy spotted me in class—how could he not, right?—and he pulled me aside when it was over and said, 'Young lady, whoever you are, you clearly have a gift for this. I want to teach you everything.' Just like that! I never paid for a class again."

"All right," Bolster said. "*Now* I have some questions."

"I figured."

"First of all, that class you taught tonight—which was excellent, by the way—had nothing to do with Ajoy's Sequence. So when he said he wanted to teach you *everything*..."

"Right," she said. "Ajoy always said that people doing yoga were like little babies. You have to train them from the beginning. The Sequence is just that: a beginning. After you master that—at least, to Ajoy's liking—you can progress very quickly. It doesn't mean you have to be good at all the poses. But he has to..."

She choked back a tear.

"I'm sorry, *had* to sense something in you, a kind of deeper understanding or knowledge, and then you can start learning the real teachings."

"OK," Bolster said. "So, in other words, it's yoga."

"We're all just cosmic vibrations," said Chelsea.

"Right. So, the other question is a little tougher. Did you and Ajoy..."

"Did we sleep together? Oh, sure, a couple of times, at the beginning. I was young and hot and stupid, and he was, well, just a man, after all. But that stopped pretty quickly. I felt like it was getting in the way of my training, and so did he. I'm sure he would have done it again if I'd wanted to, but I never pushed, and he would never have pushed me. Such a sweet, sweet man he was. I wish more people knew that."

She stopped talking then, and gazed out the window onto Santa Monica Boulevard. Bolster found himself staring at her moonily, even as he suspected that she was lying to him, at least partially. This was going to take further investigation.

"Say," she said, "do you want to continue this conversation someplace where the music is a little better?"

"Sure," Bolster said.

"I'm house-sitting for a guy up in the hills right now. We can go up there. He's got a lot of really good wine."

"Sounds relaxing," said Matt.

"It can be," she said.

Bolster and Chelsea Shell took separate cars up into the hills. He would have given her a ride in Whitey if, well, if it had been a different car. No one expected a yoga teacher to drive a Bentley—except for Ajoy, who'd had a couple of nice ones—but Whitey wasn't exactly what you used to impress, and Bolster definitely wanted to impress. An old Nissan that smelled like the locker room at 24 Hour Fitness wasn't going to do the job.

He headed up a canyon road, following Chelsea's car. She drove a Honda Fit, or one of those other budgety numbers that looked like a brightly colored suppository. Bolster couldn't quite tell the make, but it was fairly new. Seemingly, Chelsea Shell had more success than he did in this yoga business. Then again, she probably didn't have to pay for much, ever. No one bought Bolster anything more lavish than a beer, and even that didn't happen often.

As they climbed, the houses got larger, and also harder to see through the trees. They passed more private roads than public ones. That was the difference between L.A. and other large cities, especially New York. There, you lived on the streets. In Los Angeles, people were always looking for more elaborate ways to hide, like rich mountain rodents avoiding predators. Sometimes, Bolster thought it was the worst place in the world. He'd never live anywhere else.

Finally, toward the top, they reached a private drive that was guarded by a plain white metal gate. Chelsea leaned out her driver's-side window and punched a few keys on a pad, and the gate slid open. She gestured for Bolster to follow. After she was through, he gave Whitey as much gas as it could handle, and barely made it before the gate closed again, sealing them into the grounds. Suddenly, Bolster realized that he hadn't been reading the street signs. He'd followed his barely concealed lust blindly up the mountain. There'd be no trail of bread crumbs to lead him back from this gingerbread house.

They ascended the private drive for a few minutes. To the right, Bolster saw what looked like the world's most luxurious cabin: three stories of finely tailored wood backlit with various colors. He had his passenger window open and could hear the soft thrum of mellow club music emanating from somewhere on the property. Everything in this town was a secret nightclub, and no one had access.

Chelsea steered away from the cabin, up a separate road that curved around behind. Bolster started feeling a little nervous. Maybe they didn't have an actual destination. Were people going to meet them in the woods? He could use his fists, if necessary, but you could never guarantee a victory or survival.

His fears abated when, finally, she pulled into a separate driveway. There was only room for one car, so he slid Whitey in parallel, half on dirt and half on asphalt. He got out of the car. Chelsea was waiting for him.

"What do you think?" she said.

"Obscure," he said.

"Definitely."

"I was wondering if you were taking me up here to kill me."

"Probably not tonight," she said.

He looked up and saw nothing. Chelsea waved her hand in front of a little panel, and a floodlight came on, revealing a tall wooden door built into a stone wall. Ivy surrounded the door on all sides. She turned a key in a lock. Behind the door were steps, with a terraced garden on either side full of evenly spaced, nicely manicured indigenous plants, the kind of high chaparral that was L.A.'s true identity underneath all the concrete and sleaze. Perhaps it would totally revert after the apocalypse, but until that day, you had to enjoy the native shrubbery where you could.

They went up the stairs, Chelsea leading. Bolster couldn't help looking at her ass as she climbed. They got to the house, a modest thing on its own, but still way more than Bolster could ever hope for in this lifetime. It was one story, flat modernist, with a wraparound deck. Off to the right, Bolster could see an outdoor bathtub and shower, an absurd luxury.

Chelsea opened the door. Inside, it was one big room—living, dining, and kitchen all melding together—with the occasional column to divide the space. The furniture was fairly spare and angular. There was a puffy white rug in front of a fireplace at the room's center. *Big trouble*, Bolster thought. They both took off their shoes. That's what yoga people did when they entered a room. Bolster emptied his pockets, too, putting his phone, wallet, and keys on the coffee table.

"Nice, huh?" Chelsea said.

"Very," said Bolster.

"There are two bedrooms in the back."

"Whose house is this, again?"

"A guy I know," she said.

"Oh."

"He's in Asia a lot."

"Naturally."

They regarded each other.

"I'm guessing you know a lot of guys," he said.

"Don't you?"

"Good point."

Chelsea went into the kitchen to uncork some wine. She asked Bolster to build a fire. There were already logs, matches, and a basket of twigs and month-old copies of *LA Weekly*. It was the perfect combination of kindling materials. It was blazing within a minute. Bolster sat in half lotus on the fuzzy white rug. Chelsea walked over with a couple of glasses of pinot. She put them on the brick and settled beside him.

"So, who *are* you, Matt Bolster?"

"I'm just vibrations," he said.

"Nice."

Chelsea turned her back to him. She took off her top, and there was nothing but a sports bra underneath. Here came trouble.

She had an elaborate tattoo on her back. A pair of light-skinned, majestic deities—one male, one female—intertwined their limbs. They wore elaborate jewels and silks and gazed at each other with pure serenity.

"Shiva and Shakti," Bolster said. "The male and the female."

"Exactly," Chelsea said. "When their energies combine, it makes life."

Bolster could hold back no longer. He reached out a hand, which was trembling slightly, so he could touch the back of Chelsea's neck. It ran up through her hair. She dipped back a little.

"Ohh," she said. "I've been waiting for you to touch me."

"Is that right?" Bolster said.

Chelsea turned around.

"Uncross your legs," she said.

Bolster did, and then took off his pants. Now, sitting only in his yoga shorts, he spread his legs wide. Chelsea straddled him, because women could always spread wider. It took only seconds before he was fully erect. She pressed forward, her legs wrapping around his back. Chelsea raised herself up then, so her head was slightly above his. She dipped down, and their lips came together. She tasted like soft maple. He thought, briefly, that he should have taken a shower before this happened. But Chelsea didn't seem to mind.

She moved left and right over his crotch, which was already starting to ache with pleasure, and ran her hands around his chest. He had his on Chelsea's back, and slid one below the rim of her shorts, feeling the contours of her delicious rear.

They wriggled together like that for a while, rolling on the rug, exploring, giving little bites, running their toes together. Chelsea got on top. She put her lips to his ear and breathed in hard and heavy. She flicked her tongue along the inside. Bolster found himself starting to moan.

"Come for me, Shiva," she said.

"Not…not…" Bolster said. "Not yet."

"Yes," she said. "*Now.*"

Bolster felt a hitching sensation in his shaft, and he knew he'd passed the point. His scrotum tightened. Simultaneously, his head filled with light. Chelsea held him with both arms, pressing down onto him. She threw her head back and said, "I'll come with you, if you like."

"Yes," Bolster groaned.

The orgasm seemed to go in stages. At first, it seemed that it would be on the excellent side of ordinary. Bolster's thighs quivered, and he was looking forward to the end. But then Chelsea started to buck and moan and shift around herself, and she twisted in a way that prolonged it, as though she were willing his testes to redouble their efforts. A wave of pleasure overtook Bolster then, one so intense that he actually howled.

As they rubbed their yoga clothes together, Bolster felt that Chelsea Shell was soaking through hers. He felt her wet on his thighs, and then she was screaming, too. They threw their heads back in noisy union, coming hard, madly, simultaneously, and then Bolster exploded into his yoga shorts.

She rolled off. They lay side by side, sweaty, panting, and spent. Bolster felt a sticky mess running down his thigh.

"Shit," he said.

"That was a good one," said Chelsea.

"Yeah."

They lay there for another minute.

"You're a witch," he said.

"Don't I know it," she said. "You want some wine?"

"Sure," he said.

She handed him a glass. He took a sip. And then another. The wine tasted good, and he downed the whole thing.

"Sorry, Bolster," she said.

"About what?" he said.

"You'll see in a second."

Chelsea stood. She looked blurry. Bolster felt very sleepy, and then he knew.

"Why?" he said.

He tried to stand, but his legs felt like iron.

"You've been asking a lot of questions," said Chelsea Shell. Bolster saw her through a haze; she was putting on her clothes and gathering her things. She leaned in close. He wanted to reach out and slap her, but he couldn't move.

"It was fun, though," she said. "Thanks for the orgasm."

Bolster tried to speak but could get out only a "blergh."

You're an idiot, Bolster, he thought, and then he spread out on the rug, which was suddenly all he wanted out of life: to sleep on something fuzzy and comfortable. He heard a door slam, and then nothing else for a good long time.

Matt Bolster had been eaten.

EPISODE 3

NINE

———— o ————

B OLSTER WASN'T ONE TO PRACTICE *BRAHMACHARYA*, THE ancient Tantric art of sexual self-restraint. He was single, he figured, so why should he? Life was too short to repress your seminal fluids for a better, wiser day.

Still, like a paintball arena, he had boundaries. Bolster never slept with his students, no matter how gum-achingly hot they were, even if they begged him to come over to smoke weed and drink wine with them. This had actually happened once, though admittedly the student had been male—and fifty-five years old. Regardless, yoga teachers possess power, and some of them take advantage of their students. Many others don't. Bolster wanted to forever stay in the latter category. Yoga had really helped him out, and he felt like he needed to treat its core principles with respect. Once someone took his class, she was no longer sex-eligible.

But not every yoga teacher cribbed from Patanjali's playbook.

Bolster felt this viscerally as he woke to a sudden warm blast of sun on his face, that pivotal moment in the day when the marine layer dissipates and Southern California starts to crisp anew. He ran his tongue over his lips; they were crusted with saliva and hopefully nothing else. The rug felt warm and soft, and he didn't want to get up because he had a feeling that this wasn't going to be his most glorious day ever.

He opened his eyes. From the position of the sun and, more helpfully, the digital clock on the stove, he could see that it was quarter to eleven in the morning. Normally, Bolster enjoyed sleeping this late, but if he was gauging correctly, he'd been out for fourteen hours. That wasn't healthy. Bolster wiggled his fingers and toes and then stretched his arms overhead and yawned. Every joint ached from the three yoga classes he'd taken the day before. It was like waking up from the longest *savasana* ever. He'd slept like a flu victim but had absolutely no headache at all.

What had Chelsea Shell done to him? Why had he bitten from the apple? People who actually committed serious crimes wanted to stay as anonymous about it as possible. Instead, a man had smacked him in the face with a guitar and a very high-profile female yoga teacher had dry-humped him to wild yogic orgasm and subsequently slipped him some kind of weird ayurvedic roofie. Clearly, they were trying to keep him away from something. But murder? Any real killer would be hiding out in a coastal Oregon motel by now, not deliberately ruining a yoga cozy's day. It was screwy.

Bolster stumbled toward the kitchen sink and splashed a little cold water on his face. The window was open a crack, and he got whiffs of bougainvillea and pine. Birds chirped, and traffic from the nearest clogged thruway was barely audible. *L.A. would be a really nice place without all the people*, Bolster thought, not for the first time. He spotted a kettle on the stove, and he put it on to boil, figuring that he'd find some tea in a pantry or cabinet. Sure enough, the first door he opened contained some bagged Darjeeling. Thus far, the morning had been kind to him.

His cup steeping on the counter, Bolster went over to the coffee table to gather his things and check his e-mail on his phone, if it had any juice left. They were gone, all of them—his wallet, his phone, and his keys. He looked under the table and the adjacent couch, but nothing. For the next twenty minutes, Bolster scoured the house, thinking that maybe Chelsea Shell had played some sort of sorry joke on him. She seemed like kind of a trickster, not in a good way, like Hanuman, the ancient Indian monkey god that all the trendy yoga people like to invoke, but rather like the type that might get off on making a guy play hide-and-seek with his stuff first thing in his morning. But his stuff was nowhere. Then he thought of Whitey.

He walked out the front door. His car was gone. So was Chelsea's. She couldn't have driven them both out of the canyon by herself—it would have taken her two hours to make the hike back up, and plus it would have been pitch-dark—so she had to have had some sort of accomplice, maybe more than one. In any case, Bolster had no car, no phone, and, really, no idea where he was. He could leave the house and start walking, but where would he end up, and how would he get home from there? Bolster didn't even have money for bus fare. He felt his breathing growing heavy, almost panicked.

He caught himself.

OK, Bolster, be calm, he thought. *You're alive and unhurt, if a little sore. It's a nice-weather day, as usual. No one's sticking a gun in your face, at least at this moment. Every day aboveground is a good day, and all that.*

He closed his eyes and breathed in slowly, for a count of ten. Then he held the breath at the top, just for a couple of seconds, a technique that his *pranayama* teacher called *kumbhaka*. Breath retention was key to the practice. It calmed the mind and prolonged life. Then he breathed out for the same count of ten, and repeated the process ten times. When that ended, a few minutes had passed. The sun was still out and the birds were still singing. Also, Bolster was still in a shitload of trouble and was standing on a stranger's doorstep, wearing nothing but a pair of semen-stained yoga shorts. But at least he was calm.

Ten years ago, being stuck at a random house had an easy-ish solution. You just picked up the phone and called someone to come get you, assuming the line hadn't been cut. Now there were no phones in houses, so that didn't work. But having your personal phone stolen, Bolster realized, didn't hamstring you that much anymore, other than being an expensive pain in the ass. If there was broadband service, you'd be fine. He doubted that this bachelor's hideaway in the Hollywood Hills lacked modern amenities.

Bolster went inside, looking for a computer. He found a desktop model in a back bedroom, turned it on, and was pleased to find himself online immediately. He had calls to make.

Bolster went on Gmail and Skype. First, he tried Slim, who always had access to obscure rides. But Slim wasn't picking up. It hadn't turned noon, and he could easily still be asleep—and also could have decided to go down to Mexico for the week. You never knew with Slim.

He didn't want to call Martinez, who would just mock him, and besides, he wanted the cops to think he had his investigation under control. No one else seemed to be around. Then Lora Powell popped up as available. He dialed her immediately.

It rang twice, whatever device "it" was. Lora answered. Her face, looking serene and a little washed-out, filled the screen. Lora was Bolster's meditation teacher, and she always radiated calm. What she lacked in resources, she made up for in reliability.

"Hi, Matt!" she said.

"Hey," he said. "Are you busy?"

"I just took my mom to the gynecologist," Lora said.

Bolster didn't need to know that.

"So yeah," she added. "I have a couple of hours."

"Where are you?"

"Cedars-Sinai."

Close enough, he thought.

"Well," he said, "I'm kind of in trouble."

"Oh, no!" Lora said.

"It's fine, but I need a ride."

"Sure," she said. "Where are you?"

"I don't know," he said. "Somewhere in the hills. It was dark when I came up here."

"That's not very helpful, Matt."

"Hang on," he said.

He looked around the desk and in a drawer, and found nothing. Time was, everyone had a utility bill hanging around. Now they were all paid online. But a quick trip to the kitchen found some mail. He went back to the computer, and Lora was still there, leaning in close to the phone, looking a little distorted.

"13075 Fox Canyon," he said. "Number two. It's a little cabin behind the main house. Kind of hard to find."

"What are you doing there?"

"I'll explain later," he said.

"Sounds juicy," she said. "What side of town is it on?"

"The city side. I don't think we went over into the Valley."

"I can be there in about an hour. Is that OK?"

Everything in L.A. took an hour.

"Of course," Matt said.

That problem solved, Bolster felt a little better. He'd figure out how to find his keys and his wallet and his phone soon enough. Oh, and his car. He went back into the kitchen. His tea was fully steeped. It went down smooth, tasting faintly of licorice.

Bolster had some time, and the house had a shower, so he took one. Whoever lived here stayed in high-end hotels whenever he traveled, judging by the quality of sample soaps, shampoos, and conditioners on display. The shower was steamy, the pressure good. Bolster lathered himself up for a good long while, imagining all his Ajoy Chaterjee–related problems going down the drain. After a while he got out and looked at himself in the mirror. Bolster thought he looked damn good for forty-five. Then he caught himself. That was just the ego talking. He'd decay soon enough, like everything else did. Impermanence was the only true reality. Still, damn good.

He walked into the living room wearing nothing but a towel. The front door opened. There stood a man, as big and strong as Bolster but at least ten years younger, wearing designer sunglasses and holding a suit bag.

"Who the fuck are you?" the man said.

"I…"

Bolster didn't have time to finish, because the man charged forward and tackled him to the floor.

TEN

─────── ○ ───────

BOLSTER HIT THE GROUND HARD. THE SUDDENNESS OF THE tackle meant he was unable to brace himself. His tailbone smacked first; he felt the impact all the way up his spine. The guy was on him like a vampire bat with fists blazing. Bolster put up his hands in defense and held the guy off. They stayed like that for some seconds, the guy huffing at Bolster with jabs, Bolster parrying them, wondering if he was going to have to go for the knee to the groin. This guy was pretty strong, but Bolster hadn't risen to the top of his LAPD recruit class because he was a bad fighter. At one time, he'd been trained to kill. He wasn't going to lose an extended bout. But he'd also been trained in crisis negotiation, so he tried that first.

"Whoa whoa whoa, pal, hold on!" he said. "I come in peace."

The guy raised his right arm high. If Bolster wanted to, he could break that elbow in seconds, but he let it play. He'd been in serious situations before. By comparison, this was two kids rolling around in school yard dirt.

"What are you doing in my house, asshole?" the guy said. "And why are you wearing my towel?"

"I'm wearing your towel because I just took a shower. I'm in your house because Chelsea Shell brought me here."

"Who?"

"Chelsea. Shell. She said she was watching your house while you were away."

"You're lying," the guy said. "I don't know who that is."

"Look, man," Bolster said. "I'm stuck up here without a wallet, a phone, or car keys. I have a friend coming to get me in less than an hour, and then I'll be out of your hair forever."

The guy rolled off him, sat on his knees, and rubbed his face with his hands.

"I just flew back from Shanghai," he said. "I don't need this shit right now."

Bolster sat up as well, making sure to adjust the towel so he could spare the guy any unwanted vistas.

"So, you don't know Chelsea Shell."

"Never heard of her."

"She's a yoga teacher."

"Not my yoga teacher."

"You have a yoga teacher?" Bolster said.

He looked for any opportunity, even fraught ones, to talk about yoga, his favorite hobby.

"Sometimes I go to the Ajoy Yoga studio on San Vicente when I'm in town."

The guy sighed and rubbed his face with his hands again.

"I travel a lot," he added.

"I bet," Bolster said.

The guy looked at him.

"Do you want some coffee?" he said.

———————— o ————————

The guy, whose name was Brad, had excellent taste in coffee, and Bolster enjoyed his cup. Brad had also given him some clean clothes: a nice, crisp T-shirt; jeans; and a pair of boxer briefs. Matt Bolster wasn't too proud to wear another man's undergarments. He promised to return them as soon as he could locate his car.

Brad had one of those Hollywood jobs. He marketed Sony Pictures Entertainment's interactive mobile-device content to foreign media platforms, which, ten years ago, would have played as "sold TV shows to foreign countries." He was thirty-two years old, had grown up in Bakersfield, and moved to L.A. because he had some ambition and because it's not much fun to be gay in Bakersfield.

Bolster absorbed all this and then shared his side. Apparently, his story was more interesting, because as Bolster relayed the events of his last seventy-two hours, Brad sat there with his eyes bulging, saying, "No!" "You are *kidding*!" and "That is *crazy*!" When Bolster got to the part where he was having sex with Chelsea on the rug, Brad really cracked up.

"Oh, man," he said. "Would I love to have a video of *that*! It would be something to see."

"Yeah, it was pretty hot, until she knocked me out and stole my car."

"On my rug—imagine that. I should probably have it cleaned."

"I know a guy in Alhambra who gets out stains cheap," Bolster said.

Suddenly, they were pals. Yoga had that effect on Bolster's life. His relationships were so much nicer now than in his days on the force.

"I still have some questions," Bolster said.

"OK," said Brad.

"How did Chelsea Shell, who you say you don't know, come to get the keys to your house? And how did she know you were going to be out of town?"

"Well, I've been gone for three weeks," Brad said.

"Did you tell anyone at the yoga studio?"

"I might have mentioned it to Greg Vining," he said. "I take his class sometimes."

"Haven't heard of him."

"He plays the guitar during *savasana* sometimes."

That got Bolster's attention.

"Really?" he said.

"Yeah, he's quite good. And superfoxy."

"Did you take any classes after that one before you left?"

"I think one."

Bolster didn't care what this Greg Vining looked like, but the guitar bit had caught his attention. Ideas began to crackle. Vining and Chelsea Shell were in on this mess together, in some way. During Brad's last yoga class before his trip, someone had gone through his bag or his clothes, gotten his house keys, and had copies made before the class ended. That much seemed obvious to Bolster. But it would all have happened almost a month before Ajoy's murder. Had the death been so premeditated and well coordinated? What was with the safe-house concept, and if it was truly safe, then why would Chelsea Shell take a shamus up there to reveal the location? Something—many things—didn't add up with this case.

At least it was starting to get interesting. Greg Vining was going to get a hard visit sometime today, or maybe tomorrow. Bolster was a man of peace, but, like Arjuna, the warrior prince in the great Gita, he could fight hard when duty rang the bell.

At that moment, the bell rang, but it wasn't duty. It was Bolster's ride. He walked over and opened the door. Lora was standing there smiling. She gave him a hug.

"Well, don't you look nice!" she said.

Brad looked at Bolster and winked conspiratorially.

"Let me know how it turns out," he said.

Lora lived above a spartan *zendo* somewhere in the crags of Mount Washington. She had to pay only into a communal food kitty and a shred for utilities, but she made her rent through service: by cooking, cleaning, or leading meditation retreats. It was further than Bolster himself was willing to go into the yogic lifestyle, but it kept her overhead low—like, circa-1987 low.

That may have explained the ancient Honda Civic she was driving. Everything about that car was brown—brown seats, brown exterior, bits of odd brown goo that dripped from the bottom when it was parked—and Bolster wasn't sure that brown was even the original color. The air conditioner hadn't worked since Bush was in office, and the rear passenger window hadn't worked since the *first* Bush was in office. Everything, from the rear bumper to the driver's-side headrest, had duct tape affixed to it, either new or archival. Bolster's Sentra was a Bugatti by comparison. But the Civic was still alive, unlike most cars its age, and a living vehicle was all that Matt Bolster needed today.

"Thanks for rescuing me," he said to Lora as they inched back toward the flats.

"Of course," she said. "I'm all about service."

"Aren't you going to ask me about why I was there?"

"Nope," she said. "I prefer to live in the present moment."

"It's pretty juicy."

"Yogis don't gossip," she said.

He looked at her with surprise.

"I'm just teasing you," she said. "Tell me everything."

So he did, relaying everything for the second time in an hour, and Lora was just as shocked and pleased as Brad had been.

"Better you than me," she said. By that time, they were getting close to Bolster's building in Venice. He took the opportunity of a pause in the conversation to ask Lora a question that had been bothering him ever since he'd gotten into the Civic.

"Lora?" he said.

"Yes?"

"Why does your car smell like cat shit?"

"Interesting story," she said. "Not as interesting as yours."

"Go on."

"My mom had to give up her apartment to go into this assisted-living place. And the new facility didn't take cats. So she asked me to take care of hers. The problem was, the *zendo* doesn't allow pets, either. And then…"

Bolster heard a noise behind him. He looked back and down. On the floorboards sprawled a fat tabby, smacking its gums. Behind his seat was a cat box.

"You have a cat living in your car?" Bolster said.

"Not all the time," she said. "I let him go to the park with me, but he mostly just sits on a blanket. He's so lazy."

"Doesn't it get hot for him in here?"

"I'm looking for a forever home. Got a couple of leads."

Wait for it, Bolster thought.

"Do *you* like cats?" she asked.

Bolster sighed. He liked other people's cats. But he also owed Lora big-time.

"OK," he said. "I'll take him."

She smiled a little.

"I knew you would."

"But we have to go dutch on the food and litter."

"That's fine."

"What's his name?"

"Charlemagne."

"Great."

They pulled into Bolster's parking lot. There, in its usual spot, sat Whitey. On its back window, sprayed in foam, were the words "BACK OFF, BOLSTER."

Bolster was really getting tired of these people.

ELEVEN

───────── o ─────────

B OLSTER'S BUILDING MANAGER HAD A SPARE SET OF KEYS, SO
Matt got into his apartment easily. He kept an extra key for
Whitey in the kitchen, so that wasn't a problem, either. Lora fol-
lowed him up, carrying a howling Charlemagne in a basket.

"How about I just stick the litter box in the kitchen and you
can decide later where to put it permanently?" she said.

"Fine, fine," Bolster said distractedly.

Lora went about her cat business, mother hen–like, while
Bolster headed downstairs to see what was up with his damn
car.

Other than the graffiti on the rear windshield, the exterior
seemed intact, though it had been far from pristine to start. Inside,
everything seemed solid as well, and the car started fine. Bolster
opened the glove compartment. There were his original key, his
phone, and his wallet. He opened the latter, and it contained the
exact same twenty-three dollars and change that had been there
the night before. In a side pocket, he found a note and unfolded it.

"Dear Matt," it read. "There are things you don't know, and
other things you don't want to know. If you continue with this
investigation, you're going to end up very unhappy and confused,
just like the rest of us. Please, for everyone's sake, stop asking
questions. Let Ajoy's family (and the other people he cared about

in the sacred covenant of the Sequence) grieve without confusion. Please. We don't want to hurt you. Love, Chelsea."

What a load, Bolster thought. He wasn't going to let this skeezy piece of yoga strange scare him off with talk of "sacred covenants" and thinly veiled threats of group violence. He'd fought the Avenues gang to a standstill in a Lincoln Heights canal gunfight. A bunch of codependent yoga teachers weren't going to keep him down for long. It was still lunchtime. He'd be on their asses again before they could finish their quinoa salads.

Bolster took his stuff and went upstairs. Lora was sitting on his couch, watching Animal Planet with the cat. *Do cats like animal shows?* Bolster wondered. He plugged in his phone, let it charge for a minute, and checked his voice mail. There was one from Slim, letting him know that he'd be going up to Sonoma County for a few days. He usually brought back some nice treats from those trips. His mother called, too, but that would have to wait. Martinez had checked in around ten a.m. From his tone, Bolster could tell that he didn't have anything fresh, that he was just supervising to try to give the appearance of busyness. Then came the interesting one.

"Hello, Mr. Bolster. This is Arundati Chaterjee—Ajoy's widow, though I guess you can't exactly call me that, because we weren't married anymore when he died. In any case, I was his wife for many years. I got your number from Detective Martinez. He said you were handling the, as he put it, 'yoga stuff' in the investigation. Well, I have something here that I think you'll want to see. Please return my call at your earliest convenience."

She left her number. Bolster called her back immediately.

"This is Dottie," she answered.

"Ms. Chaterjee?" he said.

"Yes?"

"It's Matt Bolster. You called me?"

"Yes, Mr. Bolster. Thanks for returning."

"Sure. How can I help?"

"Well, I'd rather not discuss it on the phone."

"Not to be disrespectful, Ms. Chaterjee, but I've been dealing with a lot of cryptic yoga crap lately and I'd rather you be straightforward with me."

"Well, I'm not comfortable giving out details. But trust me when I say I've got something you should see."

"As long as you're not working with Chelsea Shell," he said.

Dottie Chaterjee laughed loudly.

"If that bitch were lying by the side of the road with a knife in her side, I'd drive on by," she said. "Or run her over."

Bolster felt the same way at that moment. He liked Dottie's style.

"OK, then," he said.

"I'm not working with anyone, Mr. Bolster. In fact, I'm not working at all. Because my ex-husband was very wealthy."

"I believe you," he said. "So when should we meet?"

"I have to deal with funeral arrangements and other things all day," she said. "How about seven p.m. at my house?"

"Fine," he said.

She gave him an address in the Palisades. He wrote it down and hung up.

"How's it going?" Lora asked.

"I have to meet with Ajoy's widow tonight," he said. "And I have a bunch of other shit to do."

"You seem stressed," she said.

"Yep."

"You need to meditate."

"Probably."

She turned off the TV. The cat mewed loudly. He really *did* like TV.

"Find somewhere comfortable to sit," Lora said. "Focus on your breath. And close your eyes."

———————— o ————————

An hour later, Bolster was back at the Ajoy Yoga headquarters on San Vicente. He'd spent most of that intervening time getting yelled at on the phone by Martinez. The press had started asking stupid questions. So far, the LAPD had kept Bolster's name out of it, but this was a global story with big implications. The *LA Times*, the *New York Times*, the *Wall Street Journal*, even the *Economist* were all up Martinez's ass. CNN had sent a crew over. It was only a matter of time before monthly-magazine journalists with a yoga background started calling, pledging that they'd give the story a "sensitive approach." The *Huffington Post* wasn't going to let this go, either. In other words, Martinez said, Bolster had better get to the core of the case, and quickly, or the shit storm would envelop them all.

Bolster could respond only that he was on top of things, more or less. He neglected to tell Martinez that he'd already had a sexual encounter with one of the major suspects, who had also stolen his car. Martinez didn't need to know that right now. His blood pressure was high enough already. That guy really needed to do some yoga.

The circus around Ajoy HQ had only grown since Bolster had last visited. In addition to the media lurkers and various curiosity seekers, a bunch of idiots were doing the Sequence in front of the shuttered bodega next door to the studio. The worst goddamn music Bolster had ever heard played behind them—an ungodly mixture of deep-throated Vedic moaning and off-key sitar. Their near-naked bodies were streaked with white and yellow paint. The whole scene resembled a cheap documentary about sacred pilgrims. It made Bolster sick. *Don't play with toys you don't understand, kids*, he thought. *Go home, sit down, smoke some weed, and have some respect for the dead.*

Bolster knew his minority opinions didn't really matter. He had a guy to see. And possibly some ass to kick.

The studio was open. Yoga cults, even ones with dead founders, don't stop going for long. There was too much overhead.

Bolster went inside. Casey Anderson sat behind the desk. Even though his eyes were as vacuous as usual, he seemed to recognize Bolster.

"Hey, man!" he said, as though they were lifelong friends. "What's going on?"

"Nothing much, Casey," Bolster said. "I'm looking for a guy named Greg Vining. Do you have any idea where I could find him?"

Casey pointed toward the main hall.

"He's right in there," Casey said. "And he's teaching in about five minutes."

This, Bolster thought, *is gonna get juicy.*

Bolster busted through the curtains without taking off his shoes. Twenty or so devotees were inside on their mats, prostrate in child's pose or on their backs, supported by blankets, or twitchily stretching their hamstrings as though they were getting ready to run a 10K, not do a moving meditation. Regardless, they all were preparing for what was sure to be a long physical ordeal. *Everything in this damn country is about achievement*, Bolster thought, *but at the end of the day, it's nobody going nowhere, looking at nothing.*

Greg Vining sat in lotus pose facing them, strumming his guitar. Bolster approached.

"Do you like guitars, Greg?" he asked.

From the look on Vining's face, Bolster knew he had his man.

"I…you…you can't be in here!" Vining stammered.

"Sure I can, Greg."

"It's against the law."

"*I am the law, asshole!*" Bolster said.

Technically, that wasn't true, but it sounded good.

"Now put down the guitar. Unless you want to try to hit me in the face with it. This time, I'm ready."

Vining put down the guitar. He unfolded his legs and stood.

"What's going on, Greg?" asked one of the students.

89

"Nothing important," Vining said.

"Class is canceled today," said Bolster. "You can get a credit at the front desk. And you can also take my Tuesday-morning class for free at Chakra Yoga in Santa Monica next week. Just say you were there when I broke Greg's guitar."

"Wait," Vining said. "What?"

Bolster picked up the guitar and smashed it against the wall. It splintered everywhere until Bolster was holding just the neck, which he chucked across the room, aiming for a spot where no students were sitting. Bits of wood and string and plastic were strewn everywhere.

"That makes two busted guitars in forty-eight hours, Vining," he said. "How does it feel?"

Vining couldn't answer.

"Class is canceled," he mumbled.

"I didn't hear that," Bolster said.

"Class is canceled," said Vining, a little more loudly this time. Still the students didn't move. Bolster pointed toward the door.

"*Out!*" he shouted.

Now they moved.

"We're calling the cops," one of them said.

"Please do," Matt replied. "Tell them Bolster was here."

They rolled up their mats and left, slowly. Bolster stood between Vining and the exit, looking menacing. He could do that if necessary. His hands rubbed together and his eyes looked anticipatory, like a dog about to be fed a meaty beef knuckle. As soon as the last person left and the telltale jingle of the front door finished sounding, Bolster grabbed Vining by the rim of his black prAna-brand muscle shirt and slammed him against the wall.

"Now then," he said, his voice oozing disdain. "Why don't you tell me exactly what the fuck is going on?"

"I can't," Vining croaked.

"What do you mean, you can't?"

"I won't."

"Dammit, Greg, either you tell me or you tell the cops. They have ways of breaking you that I won't even try."

"I'll have Ajoy's lawyers on my side."

"They don't care about lawyers."

"I can't…"

Bolster slapped Greg Vining across the face, hard. Vining recoiled appropriately. Bolster gave him the backhand with the other side. He was no Gandhi. Vining looked up, not very defiant. Bolster could see that he'd drawn blood. And he'd broken his man.

"Are you going to talk?" he said.

"Look, there was a group of us," Vining said.

"What do you mean, a group?"

"Ajoy called us the Circle. We didn't talk about it much. It's not public."

"Go on."

"Ajoy Yoga has a structure."

"Like a pyramid."

"It's not a scam," Vining said.

"You keep telling yourself that."

"You start off doing the Sequence. Your teacher watches you. Sometimes it takes a year or two to get it all right. Sometimes a little less. And sometimes more. Then, once they think you're ready, they put you on the List. It means they think you're ready for Training."

Not a cult at all, Bolster thought mordantly.

"Then, a couple times a year, teachers approach the people on their list to tell them they've been selected," Vining said.

"Selected for what?"

"Teacher training down at the retreat center in Encinitas."

"And that happens twice a year?"

"Right. For a month each time. Ajoy runs"—he caught himself—"*ran* the whole thing himself. I don't know what's going to happen now."

"And you did the Training?"

"Of course," Vining said. "There's no other way to teach Ajoy Yoga. It's a very specialized discipline."

"I'm sure it is," Bolster said.

In reality, yoga was yoga, and there was nothing specialized about it. You had to teach a few basic techniques and philosophical precepts, and the rest was just layering of style, ego, and commercialism. It was like cooking, really. The basic ingredients were there. What you did with them mattered more. It could end up delicious or leave a bad taste, could be elitist or generically mass-produced. And if you weren't careful, people could get poisoned.

"So what was this training like?" he asked.

"The best month of my life," Vining said. "It was all yoga, every day. We'd practice first thing in the morning and then spend the rest of the day up until lunch breaking down the component parts of the different poses, talking about how to teach them, how to make sure students didn't get hurt, proper adjustments, and the like."

"Sounds like the usual stuff."

"Then, in the afternoon," Vining said, on a roll now, "we'd meditate and chant, and then Ajoy would talk for hours. He told stories about his time training with Sri Charan, the trials he had to undergo, the philosophy he learned. Sometimes he'd read sections from the *Gita* or the *Ramayana* and give his interpretations. He had this reputation as a wild figure, but really, he was calm and gentle. He always took time for questions, and he made us laugh every day."

This wasn't what Bolster had expected to hear.

"He sounds like a great teacher," he said.

"Oh, he was wonderful," Vining replied.

Vining started to sob softly.

"Control yourself, dude," Bolster said. "And tell me what I need to know."

Here, according to Greg Vining, is how the Ajoy hierarchy shook out: After the top students finished their Training, they were dispatched to their home studios, wherever in the world they lived, to become assistant teachers. Over the years, the popularity of Ajoy Yoga had multiplied. Few corners of the world were untouched by the soothing rhythms of the Sequence. It had international appeal.

Sometimes, if the Training graduates lacked family or romantic attachments or just needed a change of scene, they chose a road game and were assigned to Ajoy centers with teacher gaps. Of course, that was a somewhat dangerous course to choose: you could just as easily end up yoga-wintering in Columbus, Ohio, as you could in Belo Horizonte, Brazil. Regardless, eventually you finished your apprenticeship and started getting classes to teach. As yoga money went, it was pretty good. The salary actually paid bills in some locations.

Even if you ended up someplace great, like Paris or Chiang Mai, Southern California was still the prime spot. Ajoy traveled some and had senior teachers watching out all over the world, but Los Angeles, one of the least sacred places on Earth, was the best location if you wanted the great teacher to monitor your spiritual progress. The ones Ajoy taught directly became his favorites, and that's how he came to form the Circle.

Ajoy chose a half dozen students, including Chelsea Shell and Greg Vining, to follow his advanced course. This wasn't the first time it had happened; Ajoy had multiple Sequences, at multiple levels, that he broke out from time to time, including several that were quite simple and restorative. Martha Wickman had mastered many of them, and was one of only two people in the world other than Ajoy (his ex-wife was the second) licensed to teach any sequence besides the first one. But the Circle would be different, Ajoy told the chosen few. They would go deeper. They would learn so much.

And so they'd meet, two nights a week, at Ajoy's mansion in the Palisades. It was so much different from the training they'd undergone up until then. In fact, it wasn't like training at all.

Ajoy fed them well and gave them wine. Sometimes they'd smoke a little weed. They laughed and they talked, for hours and hours, often about anything but yoga. Ajoy's older students stopped by and told stories about the days before everything got fancy. It was fun. And Ajoy asked them for nothing in return, other than fellowship.

Then one night, about a year ago, the Circle showed up for a gathering and found Ajoy brooding in his study. Normally, he seemed like an avatar of health, a banner carrier for vitality. But on that evening, to his students, he looked like a withered, defeated, little old man. All the energy had drained from his voice. His eyes were rimmed with red. His hands shook. From that moment on, the Circle grew dark.

"I can't say any more," Vining said.

"Greg. It's just getting good."

"We took an oath."

"Seriously? Because that's not going to fly in court."

"I don't care. Some things are more important than the law."

"Come on."

Vining's eyes took on a frightening intensity.

"*I will not tell you any more*," he said. "*Do you understand?*"

Bolster understood, all right. He understood that Ajoy Yoga had driven this poor dude, whoever and whatever he was, completely barkers.

"Fine," he said. "But if you come after me again, I'll break your arm."

Bolster left Greg Vining there, alone in that big, empty room, to stew in whatever private hell he'd concocted for himself. He'd find out the whole story eventually. Because he always did.

TWELVE

———— o ————

I T WAS MIDAFTERNOON. LORA HAD RETURNED TO THE *ZENDO* to tend to Zen duties. Bolster felt like going down to the beach to clear his head, maybe play a little pickup volleyball. But as he changed clothes and got his towel, the cat looked at him like, *You're not going anywhere, buster,* and then Bolster felt guilty. Lora said she was going to find Charlemagne a "forever home," but Bolster had his doubts. The roommate Bolster didn't want had arrived, along with a box of shit.

So instead of the beach, Bolster and Charlemagne sat on the couch, watching a cooking show. Bolster sparked a fatty. He snagged a notepad and started piecing together the case.

Ajoy Chaterjee arrived in Southern California as a young man and spent three-plus decades building a yoga empire based around his sweet charisma and a dubious "Sequence" that he'd developed alongside his teacher, Sri Charan. That much was pretty much public record. He had a following in the six digits, possibly in the high six digits, and had trained hundreds if not thousands of yoga teachers all over the world, doing more to popularize the practice, albeit with his own weird spin, than almost anyone in yoga's modern history. But then, in the last year, the skies had darkened. Ajoy had developed an inner circle of core followers. What was that about? Bolster wondered. From the description Bolster had heard, it certainly didn't seem like a teaching situation. It sounded like they'd mostly partied. Had Ajoy been lonely? Scared about something? Was there some weird lesson he'd hoped to impart that he hadn't revealed to his students? Or maybe he had revealed it and they hadn't gotten what he was saying?

Regardless, something had happened to corrupt the Circle. At least, that's what Bolster gathered. Finding out what seemed like the key to the mystery. Or not. Bolster didn't know anymore. Time to make some strong tea, shake off the rough thoughts, and head back out into the day. The phone rang. It was Chelsea.

"What do you want?" he said.

"Do you miss me?" she said.

"A little," he said, and he wasn't lying. "But we're not hooking up again."

"Sure we're not," she said.

"You're lucky you're not in jail right now."

"Girls like me don't go to jail," Chelsea said. "Listen, Bolster, I know you're going to see Dottie Chaterjee tonight."

"*How* do you know that?"

"Word gets around."

Shiva, give me strength, he thought.

"I just wanted to encourage you not to see her."

"Stop threatening me."

"I'm not threatening you. Just trying to help you out."

"I have an appointment," Bolster said, "and I'm keeping it."

The sutras say that you should be glad for those who are prospering, compassionate toward those who are suffering, and indifferent toward whoever or whatever is giving you a hard time. Impassivity in the face of difficult situations is the key to sound judgment. Hanging up on Chelsea seemed like the right move just then. He had to block her out.

Bolster went into the bedroom and put on some pants.

It was time to meet the widow.

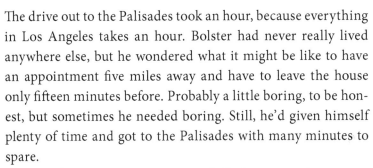

The drive out to the Palisades took an hour, because everything in Los Angeles takes an hour. Bolster had never really lived anywhere else, but he wondered what it might be like to have an appointment five miles away and have to leave the house only fifteen minutes before. Probably a little boring, to be honest, but sometimes he needed boring. Still, he'd given himself plenty of time and got to the Palisades with many minutes to spare.

The Chaterjee estate was up on a hill adjacent to other estates. The air smelled like jacaranda and fresh cuttings, with just a hint of sea breeze and a tint of leaf-blower fumes. Most of the houses lay low, like stars wearing head scarves and big glasses—not that stars did that kind of thing anymore.

Up in the chill, semitropical streets above the L.A. madness, people hid their driveways, many of which were quite long anyway, behind gates. The gate fashion had once been ornate, all white curlicues. But now that seemed as quaint, and about as appetizing, as dinner at Trader Vic's. The Chaterjee manse hid behind a wall of metal purposefully brushed with rust-colored paint that looked harder to breach than LeBron James's entourage. Bolster pulled up in front of it, wondering if his mere presence would cause nervous richies to call their private security firms. The gardeners in this neighborhood had nicer cars than he did.

He opened his front door and leaned around. Once he cracked this case and got paid, he swore, he was going to get that window fixed. In a drive-through city, your windows had to work. He pressed an intercom button and heard a little static, and then it buzzed. The metal wall drew open slowly, almost dramatically. When it was open all the way, Matt Bolster drove onto the grounds of a palace.

The Chaterjee estate was all columns and balustrades and marbled arches—a grandiose vision of pseudospiritual wealth that didn't even come close to resembling how contemporary wealthy people prefer to live. It seemed almost like a parody of a provincial raja's palace. Maybe that had been Ajoy's point, Bolster thought. Bolster half expected to see a peacock strolling among the hand-carved Ganesha statues that dotted the charmingly flowered grounds.

He rang the bell and Dottie Chaterjee answered, an attractive middle-aged woman with bright eyes, clear skin, and lustrous black hair. She wore a swank two-piece pantsuit, and it fit her well. Bolster had maybe expected a meek thing wearing a mourning sari, hair done up in a bun with a needle or something. Nope. Instead, it was just another rich, good-looking Westside divorcée. From Arianna on down, these gals ran the whole damn show.

"Mr. Bolster," she said. "Welcome to the house that yoga built."

"I would say thanks for the invitation," Bolster said, "but Ajoy Yoga has given me a rough couple of days."

"It's given *me* a rough couple of decades," she said. "Please come in."

"All right," he said.

Inside, the house was kind of pleasant, with lots of high-end Indian art on the walls; many warm, inviting colors; and soft furniture. Each room felt simultaneously homey and artisanal. Dottie Chaterjee had good taste in decorators, that was for sure. She showed Bolster in and sat down next to him warmly on a lush blue sofa. Unbidden, a servant appeared with evening tea service.

"Whoever shall inherit Downton Abbey?" Bolster asked.

"You're a yoga teacher named Matt Bolster," Dottie said. "I don't think you're in a position to make fun of anybody."

"Fair enough." Bolster said. "So what's going on?"

"Hold on, hold on," Dottie said. "Pouring the tea. Let's be friendly."

"I already have friends," Bolster said. "I'm trying to solve a murder here."

"And I'm trying to help you, dear," she said. "Really, now."

"Tell me to breathe, and I'll punch you," he said.

"Oh, my!" she said. "Those stupid children in that ludicrous Circle *have* been teasing you, haven't they?"

"You know about them?"

"Of course I do," she said. "They were all Ajoy talked about for years. Ridiculous. This was a man whom Gigi Grazer called nearly every day. He had weekly private workouts with Reese Witherspoon. And instead he chose to spend his free time with a bunch of brain-fried acolytes."

Everybody gave up good information eventually. You just needed to wait them out. *Now it's starting*, Bolster thought.

"Please go on," he said.

"It's funny," Dottie Chaterjee said. "When I met Ajoy, he was the perfect mix. He had some ambition, which was good, because ambition makes a man's blood run hot, makes him interesting. His *prana* was quite strong, in a good way, you know?"

"I do know," said Bolster.

"He was an attractive catch, even to my parents, who probably wished I'd ended up with the Patel next door, a dull doctor or engineer. But he impressed them. He was already making money, and they could see the success. It enveloped him like an aura. At the same time, though, I think he legitimately wanted to help people. There's no doubt about that. He taught me so much about yoga, and it helped me enormously. I loved him because he was kind and smart and had a little wink in his eye, like he knew he was kind of playing the West for a fool. It's a not-uncommon revenge fantasy in India, you know, which is why it happens so often."

"Well, that all sounds like a lot of fun," said Bolster. "So what happened to him?"

"When the business got big, really big," Dottie said, "so did Ajoy's ego. He started worrying about the Sequence all the time. Who owned the Sequence? Who designed the Sequence? What if someone started a studio that sold its own version of the Sequence? I wanted to tell him, 'Fuck the Sequence. Just teach yoga sincerely from your heart, and you'll have students.' But he didn't listen, not really. It got too grand for the little man."

"When was this?"

"Late nineties," she said, "when *everyone* in this town was a millionaire. People were handing him money like candy. This was a man who had spent most of his youth sleeping on dirt, covered by bugs. He didn't know how to be rich. I would come in on him in his office, and he'd actually be sitting there stacking bills, like some sort of Dickensian actuary."

"Weird."

"Then he started working with these lizards in Century City. I did *not* trust those gentlemen. They filled his head with all kinds of paranoia, making him think he had business enemies where he didn't. There were lawsuits and, even worse, threats of lawsuits. If anyone tried to even *breathe* like you did in Ajoy Yoga, his legal team was on them, like hawks eating mice. You want to know when yoga gets ruined? When the lawyers get involved. Ajoy picked the wrong business partner."

"Who was this, exactly?" Bolster said.

"Marcus Robinson," she said, turning her eyes to the sky. "May he someday leave my life."

"Do you know how to contact this guy?" Bolster said.

"Of course I do," she said. "He's my lawyer. He may have been the wrong business partner for Ajoy, but he sure as hell knows what he's doing."

Duly noted, thought Bolster. This was a potentially high-level twist.

"So, Ajoy had business problems, and he felt alienated from the world because of them, and that's why he formed this Circle? To feel like he had actual friends again?"

"That sounds about right," Dottie said.

"I can see how that could be annoying," said Bolster. "But I don't get how it could lead to violence."

"You will," she said, "when you see what I called you here for."

———————— o ————————

She took him into some sort of media room, dominated by a long, black leather sofa with curved sections. It also featured a TV that was longer than Bolster's bathtub.

"Are we going to watch Netflix now?" he asked.

"Maybe later, if you're nice," she said. "But first we're going to watch this."

She pulled open a drawer and removed a DVD.

"If that's an Ajoy Chaterjee sex tape," Bolster said, "we can skip it."

"Oh, no," she said. "It's way less interesting than that."

"Great."

She popped it in a machine and hit play.

Bolster saw an old Indian man in a garden, underneath an ancient banyan tree. And old meant *old*. He sat there in his robes, a little, wizened chunk of leather with wispy strands of gray hair, his legs crossed in places where most people over the age of seventy didn't even *have* joints anymore. Bolster wondered if there was some age at which people started actually growing roots and directly connecting to the earth. This guy looked like a gnarled tree, pockmarked by centuries of wisdom.

"Is that…"

"Yes, Sri Charan himself," said Dottie Chaterjee. "Still alive, and still operating out of that arboretum."

"How *old* is he?" Bolster asked.

"Old enough to know better," said Dottie.

She shushed Bolster, because Sri Charan was about to speak.

"Hello, Ajoy, my student," he said. "Greetings once again from India, not that you've been here lately to recognize it. I'm doing fine, I suppose, for an old man who lives by himself in a public park. It's been very hot lately, and there are many ants."

This guy throws more passive-aggressive guilt than a Jewish mother, Bolster thought.

"I'm sending you this," Sri Charan continued, "because I've been thinking a lot about you, and yoga, and the mission I sent you on nearly forty years ago. When we started, it was just the two of us in this park. Yoga was dying everywhere in the world. People in India had forgotten its traditions. The great art was going to be lost to the mists of time."

A little dramatic, Bolster thought, *but go on.*

"Then we revived it, together. It wasn't only us, of course. We were part of a wave of people who were also busy doing the same thing. I sent you to America because I knew that you were the one who could bring it back. And you did. You had quite an adventure, and I became proud. But at some point, you lost your way."

Darkness alert.

"Yoga sets traps for you. If you practice properly, it gives you extraordinary charisma and confidence. The temptations of life will flash before you like the demon Mara sending his dancing maidens before the Buddha. Thusly are we all tempted at some point. Lust and greed and envy envelop us. They play the bangles of temptation. Only by rejecting them with indifference can we achieve the higher mind. I warned you, Ajoy, but you failed to heed.

"You became selfish. Venal and materialistic. Of your sexual exploits, I do not know and do not care to know. But when it came to money and power, you bowed like a weakling. You accumulated wealth and fame, hoarding them like you were a starving man who'd found a secret stash of rice."

The old man coughed, and continued.

"Money itself is not evil," he said. "But *attachment* to it creates suffering. And when you started filing lawsuits, your attachments became obvious. Yoga does not belong to you, Ajoy Chaterjee. It does not belong to anyone. If you try to dominate it or control it, it will step on your head. And now what? Do you think it will give you eternal life? That people will remember you in five hundred years? Because they will not. You were nothing when I met you, and you are nothing now. No one is. Everything is temporary, and no mask can hide that reality.

"But it is not too late, Ajoy. You can correct everything. Each moment affords a fresh opportunity. You must teach your students the reality of impermanence, so they are equally comfortable tasting the sweet and the bitter. Stop trying to make their reality special, because it is not. If teaching them such a thing requires extreme measures, then take them. They don't understand why they're still unhappy. You need to show them that yoga doesn't make you happy, that happiness and unhappiness are illusions based on the misunderstanding of the true nature of reality."

I don't know, Bolster thought. *Sometimes people just want to de-stress on the way home from work.*

"Do it, Ajoy," Sri Charan said. "I am old. Don't let me die disappointed."

With that, the video ended.

"Wow," Bolster said. "What a dickhole."

"Is that truly one of the most extraordinary things you've ever seen?" said Dottie.

"I mean, why. *Why?*"

"Things are different in India," she said. "They take the teacher-student relationship much more seriously there."

"I get it," Bolster said. "But this goes beyond normal."

"I agree," she said.

"So after Ajoy saw this video, he turned."

"It was gradual," she said. "But yes."

"Is that why you left him?"

"No. I left him a month after the video arrived because I found him having sex with Chelsea Shell on my hot-tub deck."

"He was looking for a way out," Bolster said, "without having to do anything serious."

"Either a way out or a way in," she said. "Regardless, I got myself a place in Malibu."

"So you don't really know exactly what happened after that."

"I kept a spare set of keys to this house," she said. "So I got glimpses. At first it was a party wreck, like a fraternity had moved in. There were always half-smoked joints and half-empty bottles sitting around. You couldn't find a clean towel in the place. People whom I'd never seen before were sleeping in my children's old bedrooms."

"Skanky," Bolster said.

"It was, but I preferred it to what came after. At least when Ajoy was partying, there were lights on and signs of life. After a few months, the house wasn't any cleaner, but it was dark and lonely. Ajoy just sat in his office all day, listening to these dark chants over and over again. When I confronted him about it, he said, 'What's the point of doing anything else? There is nothing else.'"

"He was depressed," Bolster said.

"Obviously," she said. "It all started after he watched that damn video. I told him to forget about it, that it was just the ranting of a grouchy old man, but that grouchy old man had hooks in him. So I moved back in and hired a cleaning crew. Opened the curtains and brought in some fresh flowers. It helped things a little bit. Ajoy would at least eat something if I cooked. He gave me wan little smiles from time to time, and we even did a little *asana* together. But he was weak and sad, like an abandoned puppy."

"So why did you kill him, then?" Bolster said.

"I did *not* kill him," she said immediately.

Bolster didn't pull that tactic out very often, but it usually got him an answer.

"I wanted to kill him sometimes," she said, "but in the end, I loved him too much."

"You mean you loved his money too much."

"I loved the money," she said. "But I loved him, too."

"You certainly don't seem like you're in mourning," he said.

"It's more complicated than you might think," she said.

"Yeah," Bolster said. "Maybe you should tell me why."

"I can't tell you any more," Dottie said.

These people and their secrets. In any case, Bolster thanked Dottie Chaterjee for her hospitality, and for showing him the video. It was an important piece, but he wasn't exactly sure how or where it fit. Had Sri Charan's message caused Ajoy to say or do something that ended with his death? Bolster couldn't quite staple it all together. Regardless, he knew that he'd have to go to Century City to look up Ajoy's business partner. Had Ajoy shown them some weakness? Had he threatened to buy them out, or to shut down the whole gilded operation? Bad things happened sometimes when the high-rise lawyers got angry. But that would happen tomorrow, when his mind and body were fresh. Now it was around nine p.m., and Bolster was clocking out.

He got in Whitey and drove off into the night.

———————— o ————————

It would have been quicker for Bolster to take the side streets back down to Venice, through Westwood and several uninteresting West L.A. byways. But at night, after the producers were all safe in the arms of their mistresses, sometimes it was better to hit the highways. So he snaked through the hills toward Malibu, where he planned to dip down to PCH. He rolled open whatever windows he could in Whitey. The air was as crisp as an ESPN anchor's shirt collar.

He was getting closer to pay dirt—he could feel it. Unless it had been something random—and, given the manner of the death, Bolster didn't see how that could be possible—Ajoy had been murdered by a person, or group of people, close to him. At the moment, that selection came either from the Circle or from Ajoy's business acquaintances. Bolster didn't put Dottie in the safe column yet, either. Just because someone tells you she's innocent doesn't mean it's true. You don't have to attend PI University to understand that.

He drove up in the hilly, high ranch country west of Malibu, where only the coyotes and Josh Brolin lived. The road wasn't deserted—no road within one hundred miles would be, at any time of day—but there was enough space and movement for him to imagine what it must have been like here in the '50s, when a little good luck and moderately careful planning guaranteed you a slice of open road and an acre of undeveloped land. He allowed himself a rare moment to wallow in puerile nostalgia. The present moment was the best moment, because it was all you had. He knew that. It was just that his present moments had been pretty challenging lately.

Bolster headed down a steep curve and saw an upslope ahead. He also saw a pair of wide headlights bearing down behind him, far too fast and far too close. This was a two-lane road, no passing allowed. That didn't seem to bother the vehicle behind Bolster, which just kept closing the gap.

It got bad enough that Bolster actually had to accelerate. Whitey had already been going fifty in a zone meant for thirty-five, but now he had to crank the gas, and suddenly Whitey was going seventy, downhill, and accelerating. The car behind him flicked on its brights, and Bolster found himself suddenly and inexplicably blind. But not too blind to see that he was now officially being chased by a big Cadillac SUV, its grille looming like bear jaws, its V-8 engine holding at least 350 horsepower. Whitey had no skills to evade a monster like that, not on open roads like these. It was prey with no natural defense.

Through the brights, Bolster could make out a shadow leaning out of the passenger-side window. He guessed, correctly, that a rifle was involved, and swerved into the opposite lane just as a boom of buckshot rang out, peppering the road in front of the SUV. Bolster slammed on the brakes and jerked forward as the SUV shot past him. This left him in a bad situation. Whitey didn't go up hills like this very well, so turning around didn't represent a good option. Bolster heard the screeching of brakes at the bottom of the hill, and then a monstrous roar of engine as the SUV shot back up the hill with monumental power and velocity. Bolster wished he still carried a piece, but he hadn't thought that would be necessary. Until now.

On one side of Bolster sat a wall of mountain. On the other side, an unforgivable chasm. A metal beast roared toward him, guns blazing. And going back wasn't an option. Any direction he turned, Matt Bolster faced oblivion.

EPISODE 4

THIRTEEN

———— o ————

MATT BOLSTER ALWAYS TRIED TO LIVE IN THE PRESENT. That was easy to do when he was sitting on his meditation pillow, hiking in the dunes above Malibu, or enjoying a slice of high-grade sashimi. But it was more of a test when a gleaming ghetto Caddy was blinging toward him on an uncrowded mountain road while a guy leaned out the passenger window with a shotgun. The Buddha himself would have found it difficult to walk the middle path under such circumstances.

As the beast barreled up the two-lane blacktop, Whitey faced its predator with a feeble heart. Bolster rarely dared run Whitey in neutral, particularly on a precarious downslope. Whitey whirred and stuttered, fussed and whined—a purebred terrier afraid to go out in the rain, or a toddler who doesn't want to wear socks because they're too itchy. Some cars just weren't meant for adventure. Nevertheless, Whitey needed to respond, or else Bolster faced his final present moment on Earth.

The SUV, a thick obsidian block with a frightening grille, drew close. Bolster saw the passenger cock his sawed-off. He took a deep breath. A second before the guy fired, Bolster shifted into drive and pressed the gas as hard as he could. Whitey shot forward with a yelp, as though it had just received a surprise tickle, and went as fast as Bolster could have hoped. Sometimes the car could move a little.

Whitey's sudden acceleration toward the SUV caught the other driver off guard, which is what Bolster intended. The Caddy had been acting like Whitey was a parking-lot sitting duck, as opposed to a car driven by Matt Bolster, who could, if he called hard enough upon his yogic *siddhis*, occasionally manifest moments of laser-like attention. This was one of those moments for Bolster.

The shot missed. Bolster could tell. He would have felt the impact if it hadn't. As the other car sped past, going faster up the hill than Whitey could go down it, Bolster saw it hitch a little. The guy with the shotgun jerked himself inside to avoid hitting an outcropped rock. Bolster could only guess what happened next in the cab, but the passenger's move must have jostled the driver somehow. In his rearview, Bolster saw the Caddy run straight into the hillside, metal smacking rock with a sickening crunch that sent sparks down the road for a quarter mile. It skidded pathetically backward toward the guardrail, like a punch-drunk super-heavyweight headed for the ropes. The Caddy was still going fast enough to tear through the guardrail, which it did. This pride of General Motors' fleet had an appointment with the ground below that couldn't be canceled. It flipped over onto its back to begin a long somersault into the waiting chasm. Bolster didn't see the Caddy hit. The explosion he heard was enough.

Somehow, Whitey had won the duel. Bolster felt like stopping the car to give it some oats in thanks, but Whitey ate only products derived from crude oil. Bolster slowed Whitey to a normal pace, picked up his phone, and dialed Martinez's cell. Martinez answered on the first ring—apparently sober, much to Bolster's relief.

"This better be important, Bolster," he said. "I'm watching *Fast Five*."

"Yeah, well, I'm *living* it," Bolster said. "Two guys with a Caddy and a shotgun just tried to ice me. Right after I spent three hours interviewing Ajoy Chaterjee's ex-wife."

"That qualifies as important," Martinez said.

"There's a flaming pile of metal at the bottom of La Tuna Canyon that I think you want to send your guys to look at."

"Sure."

"I'm not going to stick around the scene," said Bolster, "but I'll leave my phone on until one a.m. if anyone needs to talk to me."

"Fair enough."

"Tomorrow I want to go interview Ajoy's business partner."

"Sounds good."

"But what happened to me tonight made me nervous."

"All right."

"I'd like some muscle along," he said. "Preferably armed."

"I'll do it myself," Martinez said.

Bolster liked that. It meant Martinez thought he was doing a good job. Martinez was a political animal and had a tendency to back off a case if it was making him look bad. Bolster didn't like Martinez much, but he could be a tough bastard if pressed, and he was good with a gun.

"I'll let you know when arrangements get made," Bolster said.

When Bolster hung up, he realized that he was sweating, and even shaking a little. He wanted to cry, because he'd almost died, sure, but also because he felt extremely disappointed, both in the situation, and (as usual) in the world. Bolster had gotten into yoga to escape the worst aspects of humanity. Instead, evil just crept up again, wearing a different style of clothing. Yoga was supposed to be a philosophical system that advocates tolerance, modesty, focused intelligence, and unconditional love. But just like anything else devised by human beings, it also contained the corrosive seeds of greed, lust, hypocrisy, and violence.

Who was doing this to him, and who had murdered Ajoy Chaterjee, and why? Something dark lurked beyond the field of Bolster's understanding. The mere *idea* of a "sinister yoga agenda" made him shudder. To counter that bad vibe, he decided to send warm thoughts toward the anonymous men who had died trying to kill him. It was a small thing for sure, but it was also the only yogic thing to do. Love, even for those who mean you harm, is the only true answer to all the world's problems. *I really believe that*, Bolster thought, *because yoga has turned me into a goddamn hippie.*

The lights of Pepperdine glowed ahead as Bolster started moving toward the coast. He rolled down the passenger window a bit for some air. As always when he'd just faced his death, he craved a candy bar. There was a 7-Eleven on PCH that had shelves of them. Maybe he'd even buy two tonight. He'd earned the privilege. Bolster turned on the radio.

It was playing "Rock and Roll, Hoochie Koo."

"For God's sake, no," he said.

He turned off the radio and drove home in merciful silence.

FOURTEEN

○

B OLSTER WANTED NOTHING MORE THAN TO SMOKE A ROACH, take a bath, and go to bed. But when he got home, Chelsea Shell was sitting on the bottom step of the outdoor staircase leading to his apartment. This wasn't what he needed.

"Hello, Matt," she said.

"Just once I'd like to come home and *not* have someone waiting for me," he said.

"We'd all like a lot of things."

"Yeah. You know what I'd like?"

"Tell me."

"For someone to explain why a couple of thugs in an SUV just tried to blow me off the road with a shotgun."

"I don't know anything about that."

"Really?"

"Really."

"Because that seems pretty consistent with the modus operandi you and your friends have been using the last few days."

"We're yoga teachers, Bolster. We don't use guns. And we certainly don't drive SUVs. I have no idea who would have done that to you, but it wasn't the Circle."

"That's the first time I've heard you mention the Circle," he said.

"I figured you'd know by now."

"I do."

"We have our quirks, admittedly."

"Like assaulting guys with guitars and knocking them out after sex?"

"We're just trying to protect our interests," she said.

"Like what?"

"Let me come upstairs, and I'll tell you."

Bolster sighed. *Don't invite the vampire into your house,* he thought. But there Chelsea sat, head cocked, sucking on her lower lip just a little, her eyes glowing cerulean, reflected by the street lamps. He felt himself go soft at the knees again.

"OK," he said. "But we're just talking this time."

"Sure," she said.

When Bolster had been younger, he'd often entered the nighttime hungry for love, and he'd usually found it. A good-looking off-duty cop with a wad of bills in his pocket didn't tend to spend the night alone unless that was his choice. All kinds of women took the lure. He lay with assistant DAs and bartenders, rocker chicks and sorority girls, English professors and functional illiterates. Bolster's lovers had been black, white, brown, yellow, and well-read all over. One night he was the filling in a sandwich between two Filipina blackjack dealers from the Commerce Casino; the next night he was taking an agent from behind on an upper floor of a Universal City high-rise. Rough or gentle, Barry White slow or crackhead fast, Matt Bolster had owned bedtime like 1989 Jordan owned the court in the last two minutes of the fourth.

But he'd almost always woken up feeling undernourished and a little queasy, like he'd gotten drunk and eaten at Del Taco at three a.m. The women stayed around about as long as a rented umbrella at the beach. He'd never physically hurt any of them, but he'd been cold, cruel, indifferent, and quietly seething—an emotionless bastard who treated morning-after texts like pesky flies. Even the girl who'd taken him to his first yoga class at the

Hollywood Y, thus ineluctably transforming his existence, had faded away like the marine layer. Bolster's love life was a paragon of impermanence.

Though he still couldn't hold down a relationship, yoga had definitely improved Bolster's attitude toward women. In the past, they'd been a source of stress to him. He'd considered them as potential vehicles for redeeming his shattered soul, or at least as escapes. So when they hadn't delivered on the unreasonable expectations he placed, he'd discarded them in anger. Now, he found himself surrounded by many more fabulous women than he'd ever known before. But he was able, under the banner of common yogic purpose, to see them as actual human beings, not as interchangeable accessory balms to his self-styled tortured soul. He had lots of wonderful friendships with women that didn't carry with them even a whiff of intrigue. Any one of those was worth a hundred midnight stands.

Chelsea Shell, though, was threatening Bolster's newfound peace of mind. It wasn't so much sex that drew him to her, though he found Chelsea eminently desirable. Chelsea had other, intangible qualities: a kind of magnetic confidence born from the mastery of her chosen craft, an effortless simplicity of style, and a mordant sort of wit that allowed her to acknowledge, with a knowing wink, that she understood the game she was playing. She was bitchy, and she knew it, so Bolster had to clap his hands. Most of all, though, Chelsea exuded mildly dangerous instability. In a world where so much is known and predictable, Chelsea brought a touch of thrilling randomness to the proceedings, like a human lottery. You rarely won, and when you did it wasn't much, but you just wanted to keep playing.

He felt three *samskara*, the metaphorical ancient Sanskrit "seeds of suffering," lodge in his brain just upon the sight of her. It would take a week of inversions to get rid of them, and even then it might not work. It took more than proper alignment to get over certain women.

"You're gonna be the end of me, Chelsea Shell," Bolster said.

"Maybe not me," she said. "Maybe not anyone I know. But someone will."

"You can make any cliché sound deadly," said Bolster.

"It's a gift," said Chelsea Shell, giving the cutest damn hair toss Bolster had ever seen. "Let's go upstairs."

As soon as they walked through the front door, Charlemagne started pawing and mewing at them frantically.

"Nice cat you've got there, Bolster," she said.

"He's temporary," Bolster said.

The cat walked across the living room, moaning, then pivoted and came at Bolster like a lumbering bison.

"ME-RAAAAAAAAAAW!" he screamed.

"We haven't been together long," Bolster said. "As you can see."

"I think he's hungry."

"I fed him nearly a pound of cooked chicken meat before I went out. Even a cat this enormous wouldn't be hungry after that."

"Or maybe that's why he's so enormous," she said. "Because he has unlimited room for growth."

Bolster grabbed Chelsea by the shoulder. She gasped. He spun her around and kissed her hard on the mouth. She pulled away, but not much.

"I thought you said we'd only be talking this time," she said.

"We're talking now, aren't we?"

"Barely."

This time, she legitimately backed off.

"Go sit on an ice pack, Bolster," she said. "We really do need to talk."

"You're right, you're right," Bolster said.

Meanwhile, the cat was still yowling.

"What?" Bolster said. "*What?*"

Charlemagne really knew how to kill the mood. He pawed at the thirty-two-inch VIZIO that took up half of Bolster's living room wall.

"I think he wants to watch TV," said Chelsea Shell, "like a good little American."

Bolster ignored that snide comment, so typical from judgmental yoga types. *He* watched TV. Also, he smoked pot, drove too fast, masturbated, and enjoyed a candy bar sometimes before bed. But he still did yoga, and he fucking liked it, too. Still, that wasn't a discussion he wanted to have right now, because Chelsea was going to tell him some key information—maybe. Also, he knew he had a chance to get with her later.

He turned on a show about whales, and Charlemagne immediately sighed, sitting pleasantly on his haunches. The cat really *did* like watching TV. Bolster turned off the volume, which Charlemagne didn't seem to mind. He went over to his computer and called up an old-school funk station on Pandora. Motioning to Chelsea to sit down, he went into the kitchen, took half a joint out of a tea tin, and popped open a ten-dollar bottle of pinot noir. He came out with the joint, the bottle, a couple of glasses, and a few fresh strawberries on a tray. Bolster may have been in semiretirement, but he still knew how to play a home game with the ladies.

"All right, then," he said. "Let's talk."

The Circle, according to Chelsea Shell, had a confessional aspect.

"We would tell one another things," she said, sipping on her wine. "Dark things that we'd never tell anyone else. Not at the beginning. No, at the beginning it was all good times. Ajoy said he was trying to 'forge the bonds of trust,' but I don't know if I ever really bought that. It just felt like he was trying to manipulate us."

"You think?" Bolster said sardonically. But he also found her comment interesting. It was the first time he'd heard anyone from the Circle say anything critical about Ajoy. Maybe the level of brainwashing wasn't as high as Bolster thought. Possibly, it hadn't really been there at all.

"Very funny," Chelsea said. "Or maybe he just wanted to know our secrets because that gave him power."

"From what I've heard," said Bolster, "that just sounds out of character for him."

"It was, until the last year," she said.

"After he watched the video."

"What video?"

"The one from Sri Charan."

"I don't know about that," she said.

So he told her all about the semicranky, semisinister, utterly weird video he'd seen where Ajoy Chaterjee's ancient yoga mentor had, on a cheap-looking DVD sent from India, accused his greatest pupil of perverting the message of yoga for his own greedy, shallow purposes, warning Ajoy that the end awaited, as it does everyone, and that he feared his pupil wasn't ready. It had dripped with condescension and had made Bolster very uncomfortable.

"Heavy," Chelsea said.

"Yeah," said Bolster.

"It makes a lot of sense, actually," she said. "That explains why Ajoy started calling himself a disappointment those last few months. We thought that was crazy. He was one of the most successful people in the world. I mean, who else gets rich off teaching yoga?"

"Maybe that was the point," Bolster said. "Maybe, on some level, he realized that Sri Charan was right."

"Yeah, but he didn't have to…"

She caught herself, stuttering in a way Bolster hadn't seen before.

"Didn't have to what?" Bolster said.

"Die. He didn't have to die."

"From what it looks like," Bolster said, "he didn't have a choice."

She sat there in silence and turned to watch the whales, along with Bolster's cat. At that point, he realized that he'd jumped ahead a little. *Just let them talk, Bolster,* he thought. *They always do.*

A few minutes passed. Chelsea was lit by the VIZIO's flickering gray light and not much else.

"After a while," she said, "Ajoy knew all our secrets. Or at least all of them that we were going to tell. So he said we should start making new ones. And he wanted us to do things."

"What kinds of things?"

"Bad things. Taboo things. Some sex things. He said it was Tantra. That traditional Tantric practice asked people to break boundaries so they could lose all attachments, so they could see all experience as equal. Sex with corpses, and with your grandmother, things like that."

"Yeah, but that stuff was extremely rare, if not totally made up," Bolster said. "Most Tantric ritual is completely benign."

"We knew that, too," Chelsea said. "So we drew a line."

Bolster had paid attention in his teacher training. He'd also paid attention on this case, so he dropped a question, even though it put his evening's pleasure at serious risk.

"Tell me more about why you slept with Ajoy."

Chelsea sighed.

"I did," she said, "a few times, because I thought it might make him feel better about himself."

"How generous of you," Bolster said.

She ignored that.

"We'd go upstairs while the Circle was meeting, but it was always over within half an hour. After the first time, he was no longer my yoga teacher, and by the end, he wasn't really my friend anymore, either. He was just so sad and desperate. You know how men are."

"No, Chelsea," Bolster said. "Tell me how men are."

"Come on, Bolster," she said. "*You* know. Anyway, the last time he slept with me, or tried to, is when the Circle fell apart. Ajoy was a shell in bed, barely able to move or talk. When he finally came downstairs, he called us weak and unworthy and screamed at us to get out of his house. So we did. None of us needed that kind of abuse. We left him in his living room, sobbing and alone. We couldn't figure out what was wrong with him."

"When was that?" Bolster said.

"About six weeks ago."

Bolster's job, then, was to find out what had happened in the six weeks that followed. Right now, though, he had to deal with the fact that Chelsea Shell was sitting on her haunches, scooting close to him on the couch.

"Have I given you everything you need?" she asked.

"Not everything," Bolster said.

They locked lips. Chelsea flicked her tongue into Bolster's mouth. His chest tingled and buzzed. Charlemagne made a loud noise.

"Shaddup, fatty," Bolster said.

———— o ————

Chelsea left early to teach her "Revive and Flow" class at the Santa Monica Chakra Center. Bolster slept until midmorning and woke feeling satisfied. He went down to the beach and did about an hour of *asana* in the grass. People sometimes stopped and took pictures while he did that, but he didn't care. So what if he practiced in public? He didn't have a backyard and he liked the sun.

After that was over, he made himself a big smoothie in the blender, fed the other half of the chicken to Charlemagne, and took a shower. Then he did a little Google search on Ajoy Chaterjee's business history. Everything seemed pretty cut-rate until the late '90s. That's when Marcus Robinson's name began to appear. He had a company called L.A. Ventures that seemed to have no other purpose than to skim off the top of other people's hard work and to occupy permanent luxury-box space at the Staples Center. Robinson's CEO bio referred to him as an "investor, connector, innovator, and public speaker." In other words, he was a businessman. Bolster knew the type: a legitimate con artist with a sharp nose for the main chance. And yoga was the main chance for sure these days—a $3 billion industry with an infinitely naive global audience.

Ajoy Yoga had been moderately successful for years, but when Robinson entered the picture, it quickly went global. Books that Ajoy couldn't possibly have had the time (or the skill) to write began to appear. There were DVDs, mats and mat bags, and Ajoy-branded clothes, which was particularly rich because Ajoy himself was known for practicing in a plain white T-shirt and a pair of shorts so bright red that it looked like someone had spilled cheap nail polish all over them. But Ajoy became a celebrity, so he had to sell celebrity things. He appeared on TV with Ellen DeGeneres, was a semiregular favorite on *The View*, and, in 2007, sat down for his *60 Minutes* interview with Steve Kroft. He grew richer and richer. Marcus Robinson's investing, connecting, innovating, and public speaking had clearly worked.

When he was done with his research, Bolster called Martinez, who answered promptly.

"We pulled those guys out of the canyon last night," Martinez said. "They were pretty crispy."

"I bet," said Bolster. "Any identifying aspects?"

"One black, one white, neither married, neither with any prior criminal record. They were low-key. These weren't the kind of pros who got caught often."

"I figured as much," Bolster said. "So, I need you to file for a search warrant for the offices of Marcus Robinson. Just in case we need it."

"Who's that?" asked Martinez.

"Ajoy Chaterjee's business partner," Bolster said.

"Look at Bolster, playing in the big leagues," Martinez said.

"I never stopped," said Bolster. "Let's head up to the tower."

FIFTEEN

○

MARCUS ROBINSON KEPT OFFICES ON THE FIFTEENTH FLOOR of a chrome-and-glass building in the heart of Century City, on the type of street that most people only ever saw as the backdrop for Hollywood-blockbuster helicopter chases. There was no aboveground parking on that street, only edifice, sidewalk, driveway, and well-manicured median. It was designed for businesspeople, their clients, and their employees, and no one else.

That's why Bolster had Martinez pick him up, even if it wasn't exactly on Martinez's way. Martinez was driving a department-issue black sedan with leather interior. By the standards of the vehicles that would be its parking-lot neighbors, the sedan wasn't much, but at least it looked like it vaguely belonged. Whitey was fine for going to get tacos, but in L.A., it was important for the valet to respect your car.

Bolster and Martinez got their garage ticket and headed up the elevator three stories to an atrium filled with glassy-eyed people either talking on or pounding on their phones. There was a Coffee Bean off in one corner, hosting several informal meetings that weren't important enough to conduct upstairs. As usual in Hollywood, everyone was working very hard doing nothing.

They took another elevator to the fifteenth floor. The doors opened into a lobby of frosted glass, lit brightly. Around them, behind the glass, Bolster could see shadows move. It felt like he was in some sort of avant-garde theater project about office life. They stumbled through the light to find a door buzzer, which they rang. It buzzed back, and they opened the big double doors into the offices of L.A. Ventures, which was noisy with chatter and phone calls.

Behind the desk sat a good-looking young woman wearing a sharp-looking black blouse and quality lipstick.

"Hello," she said.

Martinez flashed his badge.

"Detective Esmail Martinez from the LAPD," he said. "My associate, Mr. Bolster."

She didn't appear flustered.

"And how may I help you gentlemen?" she said.

"We'd like to speak with Marcus Robinson about the murder of Ajoy Chaterjee," said Bolster.

"Hold on a second," she said.

She picked up the phone and pressed a couple of buttons.

"Sabrina," she said. "The LAPD is here. They want to talk to Marcus about the Ajoy murder. OK. OK. Uh-huh."

She hung up.

"We apologize, gentlemen, but Marcus is on a call."

Bolster got his tough-guy dander up.

"Listen here," he said. "This—"

"It'll be about five minutes," she said.

"Oh," said Bolster. "That's fine." In this town, you couldn't even get a five-minute wait at the dry cleaner. Clearly, Marcus Robinson used the "my life's an open book" strategy. They weren't the first investigators ever to pay a visit.

"Can I get you something to drink?" asked the desk woman.

That's L.A., Bolster thought. *Someone's always offering to get you a drink on his or her way to overtaking you on the financial food chain.*

Half a glass of water later, a more highly accessorized, better-looking version of the desk girl approached. She had the same smooth exterior and placid attitude that seemed to be the trademark of L.A. Ventures. People this calm, her demeanor seemed to say, couldn't possibly be doing anything wrong.

"Mr. Martinez?" she said. "Mr. Bolster?"

They stood at prompt attention. The woman extended her hand.

"I'm Sabrina Thacker, Marcus's executive assistant. Marcus is ready to see you now."

"Enter the Dragon," Bolster said.

"One of Marcus's favorite movies," said Sabrina Thacker. "He's a third-degree black belt in Choy Li Fut."

A worthy opponent indeed, Bolster thought.

Marcus Robinson's office was probably bigger than Bolster's entire apartment, and it was certainly better painted. Photos of Marcus with all manner of big shot, including Oprah Winfrey, Tony Blair, Mark Cuban, David Geffen, Martha Stewart, Hillary Clinton, Bill Clinton, Derek Jeter, Rudolph Giuliani, Donald Trump, Barack Obama (three times), Berry Gordy, Steven Spielberg, Barry Diller, Magic Johnson, Nelson Mandela, Jay-Z, Jackie Chan, and the Dalai Lama, took up most of the wall space. In all of them, the big shots were smiling, looking glad to shake Marcus Robinson's hand. This was the platinum lounge.

Marcus Robinson stood at his desk and offered a handshake as strong as his cologne, which could have hypnotized a yak. His bio indicated that he was in his mid fifties, but he looked at least fifteen years younger, trim and hard as a post, his dark bald head gleaming as though it were emanating visible rays of vitamin D. He fit into his bright-blue, tieless suit like a mannequin.

"I want to thank you both for coming," he said, as though he'd invited them.

"You're welcome," said Martinez, playing along.

"So, how can I help you, Detective Martinez?" he said.

"Actually, Mr. Bolster here is taking the lead on this case. He's the yoga expert."

"Not *Detective* Bolster?"

"I'm private," Bolster said.

Robinson eyed him suspiciously.

"Riiiiiight," he said.

He gave a laugh, both loud and soothing, that had put hundreds of executives at ease over the years. *Just before he twisted the knife*, Bolster thought.

"I'm just messin' with you," he said. "What do you want to know?"

"Ajoy Chaterjee was murdered a few days ago," Bolster said.

"A terrible tragedy," Robinson said. "Ajoy was one of my dearest friends and one of my most trusted business partners."

"So I've gathered," Bolster said. "Tell me more about that, if you can."

"Well, I've been practicing yoga since I was a child," Marcus said.

"Really?" Bolster said. "No offense, but that means you were doing it long before it was trendy."

"True enough," said Marcus Robinson. "My mother was a student of Indra Devi's in the 1950s."

"Interesting," said Bolster.

Indra Devi was an American-born woman who studied with the great Krishnamacharya in the palace of the maharaja of Mysore in the late 1930s. She was teaching yoga in Hollywood nearly thirty years before Pattabhi Jois and B. K. S. Iyengar brought their styles to American shores. That was some genuine lineage, and not a yoga name people dropped casually.

"Yes," Robinson said, "and Mama always made us do it at home, whether we wanted to or not. Usually not."

"I know the feeling," Bolster said.

That got a big laugh from Robinson, who clearly used laughter as a primary weapon.

He continued, "I did it on and off for many years. Mostly off. But then, when I met Ajoy at a party, we talked about yoga for hours. His story was fascinating. I could tell he was the genuine deal."

"And a genuine business opportunity," Bolster said.

"Of course," Robinson said. "*Everything* is a genuine business opportunity if you look at it right. He started giving private lessons to my wife and me, and that gradually led to conversations about how he could expand his business. Mostly initiated by me. He had the business sense of a child but the personality to carry it through if properly coached. I had my lawyers draw up some documents. He showed them to his lawyers. We signed contracts, and we got to work."

"Could we take a look at those contracts?"

Robinson held up his hands and laughed.

"Gentlemen," he said, "these are clean."

Bolster had never seen a manicure that good. Also, Robinson hadn't answered his question. He made a note of that.

"Can you think of anyone who stood to benefit from Ajoy's death?" Bolster asked.

"Certainly not me," Robinson said. "I'm getting ready to dissolve the whole company. Those people he surrounded himself with have about as much charisma as a summer-camp director. None of them is fit to carry on his legacy."

Bolster certainly agreed with that. But he had some more questions.

"What about Dottie Chaterjee?" he asked.

Robinson pondered this for a second.

"Well, she certainly had motivation," he said. "And I guess she had something to gain financially, though she was doing just fine while he was alive. I don't know. The manner of the death just doesn't seem like her. Dottie's impulsive and can get angry, but she's not sadistic. She would have just hit Ajoy over the head with a pan."

Bolster and Martinez looked at each other.

"I'm good," Bolster said.

"OK," said Martinez. "But we may still want to see some paperwork later on."

"I will comply to the best of my abilities when and if that happens," Robinson said.

They stood and shook hands.

"Thank you, Mr. Robinson," Bolster said. "You've been very helpful."

"I didn't make my fortune by being *unhelpful*," Robinson said, and he laughed again. Between that laugh and Robinson's incredible scent, Bolster would have followed him anywhere.

L.A. Ventures was probably a dirty business, at least in part. Many businesses were. That wasn't Bolster's problem. But there was one issue outstanding. As he left, Bolster said, "You missing any SUVs, Mr. Robinson?"

Robinson gave a little smile.

Remind me never to play poker with this guy, Bolster thought.

"SUVs are amateur hour," Robinson said. "I like to keep my rides close to the ground,"

Bolster wasn't ready to count Robinson out yet.

As Bolster and Martinez were leaving, they ran into Martha Wickman in the lobby. He'd gone through the wringer in her Ajoy Yoga class just a few days before.

"Oh, hey, Bolster," she said. "You sure make the rounds."

"What are you doing here?" he said.

"Cashing out my shares," she said. "This place is gonna sink faster than John Friend's career."

"What do you mean?"

"Come on," she said. "You know as well as I do that Ajoy Yoga can't survive without Ajoy. Do you really think millions of people worldwide are going to practice the Sequence if he's not behind it?"

"Maybe if it works," said Matt.

"Of course it *works*," she said. "But a lot of things work. When the founder of a school gets killed, it sort of puts a damper on the whole enterprise."

"You'd think that people would rally."

"No one *really* cares about the Sequence, Bolster. Even though it's effective. People are just looking for a guru to tell them how to feel good. The party's not exactly fun anymore, and the sheep are going to start looking for another pasture."

"And you're cutting your losses."

"Just because I'm a yoga teacher doesn't mean I'm a financial simpleton," she said.

Then she slapped him on the ass.

"Give me a call sometime," she said. "Dinner's on me. Drinks, too."

Martha Wickman went into the offices to claim what remained of her fortune. Forty years of service can buy you a lot of property. Of all the people Bolster had met so far, Martha Wickman was the only one who seemed to have actually *benefitted* from Ajoy's death.

They got into the elevator.

"I didn't know you were on intimate terms with the Golden Girls," Martinez said.

"She'll outlive *your* fat ass," said Bolster.

"Probably true," Martinez said. "So is she a suspect?"

"No."

"Why not?"

"That's a good question," Bolster said.

SIXTEEN

○

A FTER MARTINEZ DROPPED HIM AT HOME, BOLSTER WAS feeling a little twitchy in the brain. There was only one thing that could calm his mind down. Well, two things, but he was just about out of weed. He needed to do yoga, and soon. If he waited until nighttime, it would be too late.

Here were Bolster's choices, according to Suzie Hahn's ridiculously specific calendar that she kept on her website: "Level 2 Kundalini," "Submission Yoga," "Partners in the Park," "Yogaluv with Spinning," six different Mysore hours given by people in their apartments, and "Yoga to Relax the Body and Mind." Bolster chose the last one because it seemed to offer exactly what he needed. The teacher, whom Bolster had occasionally taken classes from before, was experienced, sane, and not too expensive. Plus, the class was only a ten-minute bike ride away, at an unpretentious two-room neighborhood studio, mercifully gift-shop free, five doors up from the boardwalk.

Unfortunately, Suzie Hahn had also chosen this class as her afternoon refresh. Bolster was happily lying on his mat, minding his own thoughts and breath, listening to the low hum of the middlebrow *kirtan* music on the sound system, when Suzie walked in. He could hear her chirping around the room. Suzie knew everything about the L.A. yoga scene. Being part of it was her full-time job, even though she didn't make any actual money.

Bolster closed his eyes, even though he knew he couldn't wish away what came next.

"Oh, hey, Matt!" Suzie said.

He opened his eyes.

"Hi, Suzie," he said.

"Mind if I put my mat down next to yours?"

Yes, he thought.

"No," he said.

She unrolled her mat, which had thicker rubber than a lot of bicycle tires. It ran $149.99 retail, which included a complimentary organic antisweat oil treatment for its glossy surface. It was all a bit much for Bolster. Sometimes he practiced on a towel, other times on a shredded purple thing he'd found in a Dumpster behind the lululemon store in Malibu. But Suzie had gotten her fancy mat as swag after writing three short blog posts about the manufacturer, not all of them flattering. But press was press, and payola knew no bounds.

"It's really great to see you here," Suzie said. "It must be really tiring and stressful for you to be investigating Ajoy's murder."

"Keep your voice down, please."

"Sorry," she said. "I just get excited."

"I know," Bolster said.

She lowered her voice to a whisper, which was still loud enough, if you were really listening, to be heard across the room.

"*So how's it going, anyway?*" she whispered.

"Anything I tell you is going to be completely off the record," he said.

"*Of course!*"

"It's going fine."

"That's it?" Suzie said. "*Fine?*"

"What am I *supposed* to tell you, Suzie? They call them 'private' investigations for a reason. I'm alive and I'm following leads. And I can't say anything else."

"Don't be so touchy, Bolster," she said. "I was just curious."

"Sorry, I'm grouchy," he said. "That's why I'm here."

"I'm here because this class is *awesome!*" Suzie said.

The teacher, another one of those handsome, laid-back dudes with black disc earrings and a seven-day stubble, had technical skill and a clever, sane mode of flow. He gave specific *asana* instructions and only once did he say, "If you're worried about not being able to do the pose, then that's your own trip." His style was very much speed up/slow down. They did some gentle warming, then ten minutes of surprisingly vigorous poses, then five minutes in a deep stretch, and then some more heated stuff, and then back again onto the mat. They went for an hour and forty-five minutes, giving Bolster everything he could handle. He went to the edge and then backed off, as all the competent *asana* teachers advise. The *parivrtta trikonasana* really cranked his sternum.

Bolster went deep inside, gazing thoughtfully across the length of his arm toward an invisible point somewhere beyond the nail of his right middle finger. He listened to the birds and the traffic outside and the waves of breath around him, tasted the drips of sweat coming down from his forehead, felt the warm goodness of his body and the firm support of the earth. They took a ten-minute nap, and it was over.

Bolster was sitting cross-legged with his eyes closed, which he liked to do for a minute or two after an intense class, drawing his energy back inside and preparing himself for the day's remaining rigors. He opened them to see Suzie Hahn staring back at him, wide-eyed and smiling.

"Wasn't that class great?" she said.

"It was good," he said.

He stood up, rolled his mat, and headed for the door. Suzie followed him like a puppy, with quirky eagerness.

"What are you doing now?" she asked. "Back to investigating?"

"Probably," he said. "Might get a smoothie first."

"I would *love* a smoothie," she said. "But I left my wallet at home."

Bolster sort of wanted to ask how Suzie had paid for the class, but he knew her well enough to understand that she never paid for anything. "Are you going to the Ajoy memorial service tomorrow?" she asked.

"Tomorrow is *Saturday*," Bolster said.

He quickly realized that Saturday was probably a good time to have a memorial service. At the very least, there'd be slightly more parking than on a weekday night. So he added, "What time?"

"It's at two p.m. on San Vicente. People are already lining up. I'll probably be there around eight. It's gonna be a crazy show. I'm surprised you didn't know."

Yeah, well, people are too busy trying to kill me to tell me things, Bolster thought.

"I know now," he said.

Suzie had just earned herself a health shake of up to sixteen ounces, presented with Bolster's compliments.

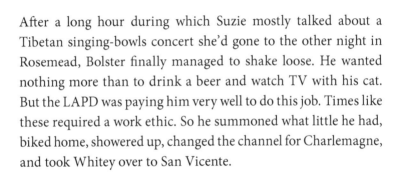

After a long hour during which Suzie mostly talked about a Tibetan singing-bowls concert she'd gone to the other night in Rosemead, Bolster finally managed to shake loose. He wanted nothing more than to drink a beer and watch TV with his cat. But the LAPD was paying him very well to do this job. Times like these required a work ethic. So he summoned what little he had, biked home, showered up, changed the channel for Charlemagne, and took Whitey over to San Vicente.

Outside, Ajoy's core groupies reveled in their spiritual home-lessness—and possibly their actual homelessness, judging by the looks of them— by lighting candles and playing the kind of canned yoga music that Ajoy, whose taste had run toward the Rolling Stones and old-school hip-hop, always said he hated. They held signs proclaiming their love for their guru, and were very busy marking one another's bodies with *bindi* and ash and chanting ancient Sanskrit prayers. Bolster could understand Americans adopting Buddhism, particularly in its laid-back Western form, but Hinduism seemed like a lot of work, with its endless rituals and a pantheon so vast and melodramatic that it made the ancient Greek gods look like the cast of *Survivor* by comparison. In any case, these were just easily duped kids who'd been swept away by the false notion that yoga's Eastern-tinged exoticism was somehow superior to whatever stultifying suburb had spawned them. They hadn't yet grasped that the "oneness of all things" meant *everything.* Bolster understood. He just wished they had better taste in music.

The hoi polloi were out there, like day-pass payers at a music festival. A few of them would get inside, but most of the space at the center the next day would be reserved for Ajoy's actual friends, for his senior teachers, and, most important, for the VIP types whose big-scale donations had made the global enter-prise possible. Marcus Robinson could bring as many guys as he wanted, even if that meant that Ajoy's beloved auntie had to watch on an auxiliary screen.

Bolster waded through the twirling crowd and went to the front door. It was locked. He rapped on it and rang a bell. No one answered. So he kicked it open.

Inside, Casey Anderson was sitting at the desk with ear-phones on. He looked up and recognized Bolster.

"Oh, hey, man," he said.

"Are you always working the desk?" said Bolster.

"I'm security," said Casey.

"Well, you're not very good," Bolster said. "I just broke the front door."

Casey looked up and saw the damage.

"Why'd you do that, man? I would have let you in."

"Sorry," Bolster said. "Something about this place makes me aggressive."

"It's cool," said Casey. "We're closing after tomorrow anyway."

"Really?" said Bolster.

"Yeah, they're shutting it down indefinitely. It's almost like someone was waiting for Ajoy to die so they could do it."

Out of the mouths of morons, Bolster thought.

Bolster mindfully took off his shoes and went through the beaded curtains. There was a power-washing crew in there, making this stinking yoga hole look respectable for the first time since 1994. In an era where big yoga studios looked more like boutique-hotel lobbies, it was amazing to Bolster that Ajoy had been able to helm his empire from this vast splintered firetrap. He wondered if the washing was really a good idea considering that this had, very recently, been a horrific crime scene. But the blood had to come off the floor eventually.

Greg Vining was supervising smugly. Bolster's face still smarted a little from where Vining had hit him with a guitar a few nights earlier. Vining was also probably hurting after Bolster had put him up against the wall the day after that. They'd been having a tough tango.

"Tampering with the evidence, I see," Bolster said when the washers shut off.

Vining looked up disdainfully and a little fearfully.

"What do you want, Bolster?" he said.

"I heard you were having a little party tomorrow," Bolster said. "I just wanted to secure myself an invitation."

"You are *not* invited," Vining said. "But you can still come."

"Fair enough," said Bolster, adding, "but I'm not waiting in line."

"I'll save you two seats. One for a colleague. And I mean police colleague, not friend. We don't want tourists in here tomorrow. Or journalists."

"OK."

"I can't guarantee they'll be front-row seats," said Vining, "but you'll be in the room."

"That's all I need."

Here they were, two men who for the previous few days had been slapping at each other like fifth-grade boys on the playground, actually having a civil exchange. Bolster gave himself most of the credit. He'd been a cop for many years and knew how to gain respect through intimidation. It couldn't be the only arrow in your quiver, but it helped.

"Do you need anything else?"

Bolster thought he'd take a stab.

"Well," he said, "I *would* like to know who killed Ajoy Chaterjee."

"I can't help you there," said Vining.

Bolster got a look at Vining's face, which was ashen. Of all the people Bolster had met, Vining appeared to be the only one who was actually mourning. The rest of them, at least the ones who'd actually *known* Ajoy—not the groupies—were going about their usual strange business with barely a hint of sadness.

Vining sat down in a white plastic chair and buried his face in his hands. When he lifted it, his cheeks were streaked with tears.

"*I can't help you!*" he moaned. "I can't. I can't."

"Fine, man," Bolster said. "It's OK. Relax. I can talk to someone else."

"He was such a sad man," Vining said. "It just breaks my heart."

Vining heaved a sob. Bolster wasn't the type to repress his feelings, but it was always uncomfortable to bear witness to this level of grief, especially from someone he didn't know. He thought he'd better leave the room.

"*So sad!*" exclaimed the grieving man.

Bolster backed toward the exit, leaving Vining to his ululations. You had to respect Vining for being genuinely traumatized, but what was behind it all? It might have been some terrible secret, or nothing at all. Thus far, the answer had eluded Bolster, but he wanted to put the wraps on this case and get back to his life of leisure as soon as possible.

He went back into the lobby, where Casey Anderson was efficiently piecing together the busted-in door.

"See you tomorrow, man?" he asked.

"Sure," said Bolster.

Casey held the door for him.

"Also, you might want to bring Vining some tissues," Bolster said. "He's having a bad time in there."

SEVENTEEN

— o —

DURING THE TRIP HOME, SHORT IN DISTANCE BUT SOMEWHAT longer in time because he had to spend half of it on Pico, Bolster mentally ticked off his suspects, on which he'd compiled quite a book. They could be divided into roughly two categories: First, you had the Circle, Ajoy Chaterjee's cadre of senior teachers whom he'd tricked into a semicultish sense of group identity and then had strangely cut loose. Greg Vining fell into that group. He was acting completely shattered by Ajoy's death. Bolster didn't think he had the métier of a real killer, or maybe he was just the worst killer ever. Bolster suspected, though, that Vining still had some things to tell him.

Chelsea Shell also fell toward Vining's side of the ledger. She'd been Ajoy's lover. Of course, now she was Bolster's lover, too, or at least he liked to think of her as such, but that still didn't exonerate her. If she did turn out to be guilty, he'd have no problem seeing her off to custody. Really, it was a no-lose situation for Bolster: get your suspect or get laid. Both had their benefits. But there he went, fantasizing again, which was the problem with Chelsea Shell. She muddled your brain worse than hash did.

Leaving the Circle behind, Bolster thought about the second category. His top two nominees were Dottie Chaterjee, Ajoy's widow, and Marcus Robinson, Ajoy's business partner. Though

Bolster hadn't looked at the books yet, and probably never would, he guessed that their potential motivations were financial, while the Circle's were probably psychological. But Dottie had already been divorced from Ajoy at the time of his death, so her sinecure was sealed. And Robinson seemed to be losing money as a result of the unhappy event. Bolster doubted that Robinson, who seemed to walk a fine line between upstanding civic booster and shady James Bond supervillain, would have made a choice so contrary to his financial self-interest, unless, again, there was something Bolster didn't know yet.

In the middle stood Martha Wickman, part disciple, part master. Bolster didn't buy her amiability for a second. She was the only other yoga person under the Ajoy banner who seemed to be able to play the yoga hustle as well as he did. She didn't have the same outward goals or ambition; fame wasn't her racket. No, Martha didn't seem like anything resembling a murderer, but her long game seemed to involve money. Bolster had been broke a long time. He fully understood money's siren howl.

As Bolster pulled into his parking space, he saw someone waiting by the steps leading up to his apartment. Seriously, he was getting tired of the guests. He'd had fewer drop-ins at a yard sale. *Maybe I should set up a drive-thru window,* he thought. *That way, people can just pull up in their cars and screw with my life however they please.*

But then he saw that it was his buddy Slim, who was perched on his didgeridoo like a border sentry. Slim also had a backpack slung over one shoulder. He'd been up north, and had a grin on his face that indicated that the pack contained ample party supplies.

"I'm glad to see you," Bolster said.

"Likewise, amigo," said Slim.

They walked up the stairs.

"What's in the bag, man?" asked Bolster.

"The usual. Maybe a little better than usual."

That's what Bolster wanted to hear.

"I'll order burritos," he said.

———————— o ————————

Slim had lived his entire life in Southern California, save an eight-month period in the mid-'90s when he'd fallen in love with an ornithologist and followed her to Borneo, where she was doing her graduate field study. That relationship, like all of Slim's romantic, artistic, and business ventures, had ended in disaster. He'd returned home penniless and stricken with a rare tropical disease. But Slim had a higher tolerance for failure than the average human. Six months later, he staged a twenty-four-hour one-man song cycle based on the poetry of Charles Bukowski, which had run for two nights before the Santa Monica community center that he'd conned into hosting him shut it down because he asked them to pay the catering bill. The show had sold four tickets total, all of which Slim had bought himself and given to a group of pier-side vagrants.

In his forty-one years on Earth, Slim had dropped out of four colleges, had been fired from fifteen jobs, and had quit two dozen more. He served on the board of directors of three avant-garde theater companies and a virtually nonexistent literary festival. His musical proficiencies included the flute, the electric guitar, the piano, the theremin, the didgeridoo, the drums, and, in a desperate pinch, the clarinet. The only time he'd ever missed Burning Man was in 2002, when a guy he knew had scored him a spot in a luxury box at the US Open. Unfortunately, the truck he'd taken to New York as part of a drive-away program had broken down outside of Knoxville, and he'd ended up spending the week working in a Waffle House instead, which he later called "the most spiritual experience of my life."

When it came to yoga, Slim was no shirker, either. He'd studied in Rishikesh, Mysore, Pune, Chennai, and Mendocino.

He could do a fully expressed one-legged wheel while wearing a peacoat and crusty old jeans, and could meditate for two hours without twitching. He was a strict vegetarian and drank wine only on ceremonial occasions. Of course, he also slept eleven hours a day and did more drugs than the 1987 New York Mets had done in their combined prime. No one lived in the moment more thoroughly than Slim. Thus far, he'd survived.

Bolster and Slim went back a few years, dating to the time when Bolster had slipped into the L.A. yoga scene unnoticed after his police career hit the shoals. Slim had sensed in Bolster someone with a similar affinity for extended leisure time on a low budget. It wasn't a relationship that Bolster wanted to over-emphasize. Though he drifted through life like a liter soda bottle on the waves, Slim always had plans and schemes, too many for Bolster, who preferred to streamline. Slim tended to bring drama. If you gave him too much rope, you could end up getting hung. But for a casual hang after a stressful day, he was the greatest.

"Where you been, Slim?" Bolster said, as they headed up the stairs.

"Sonoma," Slim said. "Shit got real."

The only "shit" Bolster could imagine "getting real" in Sonoma County, one of the wealthiest, most rarefied tracts on Earth, was artisanal wine production, but he was sure that Slim had a story. Slim always did. They opened the door. Bolster's living room smelled sour. At that moment, he remembered that he had a cat.

"ME-RAAAAAAAAAAW!" Charlemagne howled as he charged toward Bolster, anger in his eyes.

"What the fuck is that thing?" Slim said.

"It's temporary," Bolster said.

"I hope so."

"Lora's mom had to move into a home, and it was living in Lora's car."

"So you got it?"

"I had the space," Bolster said.

Charlemagne continued his loud protesting.

"I think he's hungry," said Slim.

Bolster looked into the apartment. Beams of dusty light shot through the half-opened patio door shades. The TV was off.

"Nah, he accidentally sat on the remote," Bolster said.

They went inside. Slim put down his backpack. Bolster turned on the TV. Turner Classic Movies was showing *How Green Was My Valley*. Again. Charlemagne heaved himself up onto the sofa and settled on his haunches, purring softly.

"He likes TV," Bolster said.

Slim opened up his backpack and pulled out two huge bricks of *Cannabis sativa*, triple vacuum-packed for optimal freshness. Bolster secretly preferred the days when cops who filched from the evidence room got most of the good weed. The golden age of medical marijuana, if you were a seventeen-year-old kid from Boyle Heights or the pastor of a storefront church located next to a pot shop on Fountain, had its detriments. But a guy like Bolster, who ran almost no risk of ever going to jail, was in stoner heaven.

"Whoa," Bolster said. "Is that for me?"

"Not all of it," said Slim. "I've got to pay my bills. But you can have a snack."

Slim pulled out a third bag, smaller than the first two but still containing more marijuana than Bolster could possibly consume in a year.

"Wow," Bolster said. "Thanks."

"To celebrate a successful investigation," said Slim.

"It's not successful yet," Bolster said.

"All the more reason to give it a try."

Bolster opened the bag a crack. It smelled intoxicatingly of limes and faintly of ass. Ah, sweet sinsemilla!

"Let's vaporize this shit," he said.

Meanwhile, somewhere near Bolster's apartment, shadows lurked at sundown.

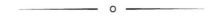

An hour later, Charlemagne had passed out from the second-hand vapor and Bolster wasn't far behind him. It had been a tough few days. He'd been hit in the face with a guitar, drugged, and been caught in a deadly car chase, with guns. Plus, he'd done about a half dozen *asana* classes. Bolster had earned this Friday night.

On the other hand, Slim, whose entire life was a state of rest, had lots of energy. He sat in Bolster's easy chair, waving his hands excitedly and talking about the trip he'd just taken up north.

"So I get there," he said, "and this dude has a full greenhouse set up out back, rows and rows of all kinds of plants. They're stacked in rows all the way up to the roof. The same thing in his garage, which could easily hold four cars. The thing is, he's not doing this out in the country. It's this really nice suburban neighborhood where successful doctors and retired tech executives live. I was like, 'Dude, you can't do this—you're gonna get in trouble.' He said, 'I'm only here for six months, until the guy who owns this house gets back from Switzerland.'"

"Sounds like trouble," Bolster said. "If *you* think someone's showing bad judgment, then they've got a real problem."

"Seriously," said Slim. "So I crash there, and then there's an electrical short in the greenhouse. The weed catches on fire. This dude is out there with an extinguisher, but the flames are getting pretty intense and the air really starts smelling like some serious dope. I hear sirens, and I'm like, 'Fuck this. I don't care if it's the middle of the night—I'm going to the bus station.' It took me two days to get home, but only because I stopped at Hearst Castle on the way. That place trips me out."

Bolster sprawled, breathed, and rallied. He got up.

"Hey, man," he said, "let's go down to the beach and watch the sun set. It'll be very romantic."

"I'll meet you there," Slim said. He stood up and started walking toward the bathroom fast, emitting a tough-sounding grunt on the way. Bolster didn't want to know any more.

He went down to the ocean. It had been a hot day, but now the air felt as refreshing as a cool bottle of ginger beer. Kids on skateboards whizzed past, as kids had been doing down here for decades. People of all ages, shapes, sizes, ethnicities, and gender identities strolled the boardwalk, living their dramas, listening to their private music. The beach was the net that caught all the human flotsam drifting out to sea, and Bolster loved it so.

The sutras say that suffering is universal, but that a thorough self-investigation into the causes of that suffering can make it at least tolerable, if not totally better. Bolster felt that strongly on this Friday night. He was grounded and optimistic, full of life and possibility, a man doing right and still in his prime. After the week he'd had, most people would be scared out of their minds, and with good reason, but Bolster didn't play the paranoia game. Sure, he needed to be cautious, but he couldn't help himself. He had a semipermanent case of "yoga brain," which made it hard for him to feel bad, or scared, or angry for any extended length of time. Bolster walked through the world on self-styled lotus feet. Maybe that got him into trouble, but it was how his brain worked, and he felt no need to change.

This is some seriously good weed, he thought.

Bolster strolled over to the weight-lifting area, always his favorite spot. He spent a lot of time over there, not because he loved to watch guys lifting weights, necessarily, but because of the characters who hung around there, like the old black man in a wizard hat who watched closely, muttering stuff like, "That's a clean jerk. That's a clean jerk."

When Bolster arrived, he noticed that the usual wackos had cleared out. Instead there were five dudes—all wearing black sweatpants and black muscle shirts, all of them with close-cropped hair, and all of them built like ball-peen hammers—who were just pounding the free weights, gleaming with sweat, with nothing even close to a smile anywhere near their face. Bolster looked at one of them and got a glare that could have stopped an ice-cream truck.

These are not your people, Bolster, he thought to himself. *Walk on.*

Bolster took off his flip-flops and walked onto the sand, refreshingly free of cigarette butts these days. He took a big inhale of sea air and felt deliciously alive. Behind him, he heard a loud *clang!* and then another.

One by one, the muscle heads put down their weights and dramatically vaulted themselves out of the lifting area. Two of them exited to the left, three to the right. They were walking toward the beach, specifically toward Bolster, and were doing so with Terminator-like efficiency, forming a phalanx of cruel muscle. Bolster knew danger when he saw it, and this was dangerous indeed.

Another sutra goes: "Suffering that hasn't been created yet can be prevented." But when you're Matt Bolster, even getting stoned and going out for a walk can lead to suffering. He was about to find out just how much.

Bolster clenched both fists, inhaled, and prepared for the worst.

EPISODE 5

EIGHTEEN

———— o ————

THE LIFTERS WERE CLOSING IN FAST. MATT BOLSTER ESTI-
mated he had fifteen seconds, maybe twenty, before the
five-man phalanx of premium beef reached him. Adding maybe
a minute—about how long it would take them to smash in his
brain—that was all that remained of Bolster's time on Earth,
unless something changed immediately. It was pretty obvious
that they weren't looking to recruit him for their pub-trivia team.
These hulks wanted to smash.

But the sand appeared to be slowing them down a little.
Fortunately, Bolster knew how to move in sand. He'd played a lot
of beach volleyball since he'd retired from the force.

He feinted left. The musclemen hitched just enough. Bolster
dashed right, running back up toward the boardwalk on a diag-
onal. That bought him about five seconds. He whipped out his
phone and tried to send Martinez a text, typing fast and inaccu-
rately. The copy was supposed to read: *Being attacked at Muscle
Beach. Send help.* Instead, it came out as: *Beings attached at
Myrtle Beach. Syrup.*

Stupid autocorrect.

Bolster sent it anyway.

He cut left toward the weight-lifting area. Maybe someone
there would help him, though that was a small chance. L.A.

wasn't exactly teeming with citizen heroes. If you had something to offer them, its people would do anything for you. Otherwise, you were screwed.

Bolster saw that his assailants were starting to pant. So was he, though, and they were a lot younger and stronger. In a back-bending contest, he'd beat them no problem, but they had every other physical advantage besides flexibility. They were intending to bend him further than was helpful. Even the supplest spines can snap.

Oh shit oh shit oh shit, Bolster thought inelegantly.

One of the guys lunged, catching Bolster by the ankle. Bolster hit the sand, feeling something give a little in his shoulder. The guy sprang to his feet and cocked back. Bolster got ready for ultimate impact. Intellectually accepting the reality of imper-manence is one thing. Actually dealing with it when it comes knocking for you is quite another. He wasn't ready to die.

Out of nowhere came this sound: "*Heeeeee-yaaaaaaah!*"

A lacquered stick, eight feet long and eight inches thick, thwacked Bolster's first assailant across the head, sending him sprawling. At the other end of the stick stood Bolster's buddy Slim, looking ready. Slim was the only man in North America, Bolster guessed, who could powerfully wield a didgeridoo. Normally, Slim played his didge at poorly attended coffeehouse concerts around town. But his martial-arts studies had included quite a bit of weapons work, which apparently applied to anything long and wooden. The present moment had suddenly turned in Bolster's favor.

"Make new friends but keep the old," Slim said.

"You sure you want to do this?" said Bolster. He got to his feet.

"I can handle it," said Slim. "I've been training."

Two guys were charging straight at Slim, ready to throw him out of the way. Slim twirled the didge, smacking one in the face, sending him sprawling. Swooshing down, he hit the other guy hard with the backlash. The second guy took it straight in the gut. He fell to his knees with a gasp.

"Thanks for playing," Slim said.

The remaining two guys reached the scene. Their deltoids, pasted with incomprehensible tattoos, were bursting out of their muscle shirts. Bolster dodged a fist, feeling it burn across his right ear. It hurt, but this was no time to whine. He threw a counterpunch, which totally whiffed. Hand-to-hand combat wasn't going to win here. Bolster returned to strategic-evasion mode. He ducked under the railing into the weight-lifting area. The guys followed.

Muscle Beach was a throwback to the old days of *Pumping Iron*, before climbing walls and Jacobs Ladder gym machines, when exercise was exercise and running a marathon wasn't some sort of civic accomplishment to be trumpeted on Facebook. No one did isometric lunges here. There were no boot camps for stressed-out PR executives. Most important, this wasn't a yoga place, and Bolster was grateful. Otherwise, he'd have to defend himself with eight-inch-thick foam blocks and canvas straps with plastic buckles. Instead, he got behind a rack and started chucking five-pound weights at his assailants. They swatted the weights away like so many pesky bugs, but a couple landed, one on a chest, one on a thigh. Even for guys with this much padding, that must have left bruises.

Finally, though, they cornered Bolster. He had to engage. Bursting forward, he went for the midsection of the closest one, a buffed-out, do-ragged, pencil-mustached dude who was at least something close to Bolster's width. The surprise attack sent the guy to the mat, but he quickly rolled Bolster over and started nailing him with fat blows to the middle. Bolster put his hands up, trying to dodge and weave on his back, but this dude clearly had punching experience.

Off to Bolster's right, Slim planted his didge in the sand like he was pole-vaulting. Slim rose up and side-kicked one of the guys into oblivion. He slid down, stood upright, whipped up the didge again, and, with a fast back-and-forth double chop, knocked the other two guys down for good.

People had gathered on the boardwalk. They were starting to take videos. This gave Bolster motivation. He didn't want Slim showing him up. The world needed to see that Matt Bolster could dish out the pain.

Bolster slid away and stood up, already feeling the bruises forming in his middle and something that kind of felt like a fractured rib. He grabbed a weight-lifting bar from its holder and swung. It missed everything, came back around, and hit Bolster in the back of the head. He bit his tongue, spat out blood, and went down to his knees. Slim appeared alongside him.

"Leave it to the pros, Bolster," he said.

Two swings of the didge, a quick punch with his left, and Slim had these two guys down as well.

I'm gonna have to put Slim on the payroll, Bolster thought.

Bolster had an ostrich egg blooming on the back of his head and a slight burn on the left side of his chest, but he rallied. One of the guys was squirming on the deck. Bolster went over, straddled the guy, and slapped him across the face.

"Wake up," Bolster said.

He slapped him in the other direction.

The guy blubbered and shook. His eyes looked gray and hazy. Slim's didgeridoo had really packed some torque.

"Who sent you?" Bolster said.

The guy spat at Bolster's face. Bolster dodged but still got some spray. It was sticky and specked with blood. He slapped the guy again and nodded toward Slim. On command, Slim grabbed the didge with both hands, poising it over the guy's forehead.

"He's earned the right to pile drive," Bolster said. "Now, I recommend that you answer my question."

The guy was still silent.

"*Who sent you?*" Bolster shouted.

Slim brought the didge down with maximum force. The guy shrieked. Bolster threw up a hand, and Slim stopped just before impact.

"Marcus Robinson," the guy blubbered.

Ajoy Chaterjee's business partner was apparently in the thug-hiring business. Bolster guessed he'd sent the SUV of death the night before as well. But now another platoon of Robinson's army had been vanquished. Amateurs.

"Did he say why?" asked Bolster.

"No. We were supposed to go up to your apartment at sunset, but when we saw you outside, we thought we'd get a jump."

"Looks like your jump got jumped, pal!" Slim said.

Bolster needed to instruct Slim about not gloating. Even a high-end didgeridoo ninja wasn't going to win every time. Don't get attached to results.

The cops had shown up by now. They were busy subduing Bolster's attackers one by one. Martinez was with them. He entered the weight-lifting area.

"That was fast," Bolster said.

"I got your text," he said. "Myrtle Beach is lovely this time of year."

"Fuck off," Bolster said.

"Who knew that yoga people were so violent?" said Martinez.

"There's no such thing as yoga people," said Bolster. "There are just people and yoga. And yoga is everywhere, whether people 'do' it or not."

Martinez didn't look impressed by this profound observation. Bolster needed to give him something useful.

"They work for Marcus Robinson," said Bolster. "We need to bring him in, assuming we can get past his bodyguards and his lawyers."

"When?"

"As soon as possible."

"You think he did Ajoy?"

"He wouldn't keep sending guys to kill me over an unpaid speeding ticket," Bolster said.

On the beach, as the cops hauled away the guys Slim had smacked around, Slim was turning didgeridoo tricks for the tourists. Bolster wanted him to wrap it up already. Behind them, the sky was exploding in streaks of purple and red and orange. The day said good-bye in the usual L.A. manner, flashy but distant.

"Nice sunset," said Martinez.

"Yeah," said Bolster, "but that means only twelve hours until the dawn."

NINETEEN

———— o ————

MARCUS ROBINSON LIVED IN SHERMAN OAKS, SOUTH OF Ventura, up in the hills, a neighborhood where undocumented Mexicans gas-blew leaves all day and the coyotes roamed for real all night. His neighbors were plastic surgeons, real-estate flippers, and sitcom writers and actors who'd gotten lucky enough to work on something that had gone into syndication. For most people, a three-thousand-square-foot home overlooking the San Fernando Valley was an unreachable dream. But Marcus Robinson was merely slumming it up there. He saved truly high-style neighborhood living for his vacation homes.

Bolster, Slim, and Martinez pulled up around eight p.m. The house had a circular stone driveway flanked by drooping eucalyptus and walls of rosebushes, which were lovingly trimmed twice weekly by faithful, high-paid arborists. They had to park on the street because the driveway was occupied by a Fisker Karma, a Rolls-Royce Ghost Coupé, and a black Mercedes SUV that looked suspiciously like the one that had tried to run Bolster off a canyon road and into Malibu Creek the other night. To the left was a three-car garage, doors shut tight. Bolster wondered if that was where Robinson kept the cars he actually drove.

The driveway was well lit, and there was a lot of light coming from the inside, too.

"*Someone's* home," said Martinez.

"Sharply observed, Detective," said Bolster.

"Right."

They got out of Martinez's car, Slim exiting last from the backseat. He'd napped the whole way, flush with victory. Bolster hadn't wanted Slim to come along, but after his display on the beach, Slim answered to no one. Bolster supposed Slim provided some intimidation of the weird Criss Angel variety. He was the baddest ass at the poetry slam.

"Leave the didgeridoo," Bolster said.

"No way, man," said Slim. "The didge goes where I go."

Suddenly, Slim was posing like Gandalf for real. Bolster hoped this phase ended soon.

"Fine," Bolster said. "But if you break anything, I'm taking it away from you."

"OK, Dad," said Slim.

The house was a garish two-story job, all frosted glass and yellow stone—materials that cost a lot, melded poorly with the landscape, and looked great under the glare of strategically placed dinner-party lawn lights. They walked up and rang the bell. A few seconds passed, and then Bolster heard, "Daddy! Someone's at the door!"

"Answer it, please!" Bolster heard Robinson shout.

"I can't!" shouted the kid. "I have to go poop!"

Here Bolster had come in expecting Scarface, and he'd gotten Cosby.

A few seconds later, Marcus Robinson answered the door, looking casual but still totally sharp in a brightly colored designer golf shirt and pressed khakis.

"Mr. Bolster, Detective Martinez," he said, as though he'd been expecting them. "How can I help you?"

Bolster kept his voice low.

"You can start," he whispered, "by explaining why you keep sending guys to kill me."

"I don't know what you mean."

"There's five men locked up right now in Santa Monica who would testify otherwise."

Robinson's expression changed, but only slightly.

"I'll stop," Robinson said, "if you stay away from me."

"I'm trying to find a killer," said Bolster, "and I'm thinking it might be you."

"Bolster," said Robinson, "I ain't your damn killer. But I have affairs I need to protect."

"I don't work for the SEC," Bolster replied. "But until I figure out what happened to Ajoy Chaterjee, you'd better keep the books wide open. And you're coming with us. Right now."

From inside, Bolster heard, "Hey, Marcus. Everything OK?"

That voice sounded familiar to Bolster. Too familiar. Almost like he'd been hearing it his entire adult life.

Robinson opened the door wide.

"Mr. Bolster," he said, "have you met Magic Johnson?"

There sat the great Magic on Marcus Robinson's couch, famous smile gleaming. He stood up, walked forward, and extended a meaty mogul's hand. Bolster and Martinez tried to play it cool, but Slim gaped like he'd just seen Santa Claus.

"Oh, sweet Lord in heaven," Slim said.

"Gentlemen," Magic Johnson said, "it is my pleasure."

"These gentlemen are helping with security for Ajoy's memorial service tomorrow," Robinson said.

"Such a terrible thing," Magic said. "Ajoy was my yoga teacher, and a wonderful man."

"Ajoy was your yoga teacher?" Bolster asked.

"The three of us studied together every Sunday for almost twenty years," Marcus Robinson said.

"A dear friend and business partner," said Magic.

"Business partner?" said Bolster.

"Ajoy, Magic, and I had many business interests together," said Robinson. "I handled the legwork, but Magic did a lot of the investing."

Robinson looked at Bolster and Martinez slyly, as if to say, *If you arrest me now, you also have to arrest Magic Johnson.* Or at least embarrass him. Magic wasn't on the suspect list, or any suspect list, ever. And he wouldn't be unless the LAPD wanted to deal with a media shit storm the size of the O. J. trial crossed with Michael Jackson's death times topless Kate Middleton. No one else on the planet could play a trump card like this one; Robinson was good.

"Well then," Martinez said.

"So I trust everything is OK security-wise tomorrow?" Robinson said.

"It's fine," Bolster said through gritted teeth.

"You gentlemen didn't have to come all the way out here just to tell me that."

Stop taunting me, you smug ass, thought Bolster.

"Excuse me, Mr. Johnson?" asked Slim.

"Call me Magic, my strange goth friend," said Magic Johnson.

"Could you autograph my didgeridoo?"

"Sure thing," Magic said.

Don't ask him out for tacos, Slim, Bolster said to himself.

"You want to go get tacos afterward?" Slim said.

Magic Johnson didn't accept Slim's offer to go get tacos. Instead, he had Marcus Robinson's black Mercedes SUV take him to Dodger Stadium. He watched the game from the owner's box behind home plate, a privilege he'd deeply earned.

"He was actually kind of rude about it," Slim said later, in the car.

"Dude, what did you expect?" said Bolster. "Magic Johnson is not going to have tacos with you."

"I had tacos with Henry Rollins once," Slim said.

"That's not the same thing," said Bolster.

After a few minutes of whining, Slim lapsed into a mopey backseat silence. Martinez, always happy not to talk, joined him. Meanwhile, Bolster found himself a little mentally adrift, though he would never have admitted it to Martinez, the man who controlled the distribution of his current payday. At every step since he'd taken on this investigation, people had been trying to do Bolster harm. Yet none of these people appeared to be hiding anything pertinent. It was as though Ajoy Yoga had driven them all crazy. Maybe yoga had driven *him* crazy. Or maybe the world operated without any truly set principles. Things just bounced off other things, weaving imperceptible patterns of activity into a cruel, impossible-to-navigate, joke landscape. The point of a yoga practice, or at least one of its purposes, was to clear your mind so you could discern those patterns intelligently.

It looked like Matt Bolster was going to have to practice a little harder.

On the morning of Ajoy Chaterjee's memorial service, Bolster did yoga in his living room. He'd decided to stay in after the previous evening's beach debacle. The marine layer had stuck around all morning, making the air chilly and misty. It was no fun to practice on a damp mat unless your sweat was causing the dampness. Better to stay indoors with partially working central heat.

After a few days on this case, Bolster had more than his share of "contusions," as the horribly overwritten police reports said. They weren't contusions. They were *bruises*. Whatever they were, Bolster had been knocked around pretty hard. So of course he had to keep practicing. When life presents its greatest difficulties, that's when you need yoga the most. As always, yoga made him better.

Most of us move through our lives in a perpetual fog, trapped in an amorphous cycle of misunderstanding and mental confusion.

But through some miraculous combination of circumstance and hard work, Bolster thought he'd found a way out, a surprise, midlife escape pod. By existing in the present moment, by seeing reality for what it truly is—a beautifully ephemeral and constantly changing miracle—Bolster had discovered that he could, at least temporarily, unlash his soul from *samsara*, the great cosmic wheel of suffering that cruel fate has burdened us to push around forever.

When Bolster first started practicing yoga, nearly a decade before, everything was so simple. He had his breath and his body. Everything else was just spaces in between. Yoga took him to a place—encompassingly universal but also deeply personal—that transcended the human nonsense, ambient noise, mental distraction, and superficiality that clouds our daily lives.

Bolster well understood the fruitlessness of most endeavors, the walking wastes that people's lives become—sometimes by their own doing, sometimes at the hands of others, and often just through the cruel, random inevitability of life and the fate that awaits us all. By the time Bolster found yoga, he was already broken, his ego shattered by hard living and by witnessing too much violence, poverty, and injustice. As a yoga teacher, he thought if he could alleviate even a small amount of suffering for just a few people, then he'd be doing all right.

Unfortunately, yoga plays tricks.

At the beginning of his yoga life, Bolster was as innocent as a kindergartner. The political alliances and petty commercial disputes of the yoga world might as well have belonged to a foreign country. Only gradually, heartbreakingly, did Bolster realize that yoga people were just as screwed up as everyone else, sometimes even more so. People developed skills, mental and physical, that previously had seemed impossible to them. Some took those skills and gently pushed them into the background as a supplement to a full, engaged life off the mat. Often, though, they exaggerated their new talents, showed off, cashed in, and blew up their egos like car tires left on the air pump too long.

On a small scale, this could lead to injuries and disappointment, and a sad abandonment of yoga's very real benefits. Writ large, it could lead to cults. Yoga had become a lifestyle drug for the privileged and deluded.

Bolster pushed himself hard on the mat that morning, probably harder than necessary. But sometimes a gentle practice just didn't help him. He went through a vigorous *vinyasa* routine, jumping back into *chaturanga* after every pose, his breath sounding like a laptop cooling fan. Always staying mindful, he bumped up against his edge but never pushed past, trying to remember that this was a workout, not a punishment. A little soreness was fine, but even a small amount of pain was bad, or at least unnecessary. Yoga was supposed to make you feel good.

This hamstring ain't gonna stretch itself, he thought, wrenching himself into yet another triangle pose.

He went upside down for five minutes, folding his hands behind his head, keeping his elbows close together, distributing the weight as evenly as possible among the crown, his wrists, and his forearms, taking care not to compress his neck, breathing in for a count of five and out for a count of five, repeating this sixty times. Then he moved back into child's pose for a bit, giving it as much care as he could. The calming, ordinary counterpose is just as important as the awesome-looking one that requires a lot of outward effort. Yoga teaches us to breathe into the mundane.

Next, Bolster went legs up the wall, scooting his butt flush against the floorboard. His forehead dripped fat beads of sweat onto the mat. A delicious cooldown period had arrived. Bolster breathed there for a while, then returned to his mat for a few simple bridge poses, pigeon on both sides to relax the hips, some simple supine spinal twists, and then, mercifully, *savasana*, the rest beyond rest.

He felt the *prana* pulse through his feet, up through his ankles and legs. Then it was filling his entire body with a warm tingle. No one had ever been able to sufficiently explain to Bolster what *prana* represents. Was it an advanced response of the nervous system, or maybe the eternal song of the universe vibrating in our marrow? Either way, or some other way, *prana* was the most ecstatic thing knowable, part full-body orgasm, part acid trip, part homecoming to the happiest moments of childhood innocence. It was yoga's greatest gift, and also its greatest curse, because *prana*, like everything else, is impermanent. When the sensation dissipates, you have to let it go and not expect it to turn up at any particular time. Too much grasping for ecstasy leads to evil deeds.

For now, though, Bolster felt damn good, like he was taking a warm shower on a cold day. He drifted, his thoughts far away from Ajoy Yoga, from everything and everyone who had plagued him this week. Thoughts passed through his brain and he watched them without judgment. Most likely, he also slept.

He heard the faint ringing of a Tibetan singing bowl, a zipping sound followed by a louder, fuller strike. Teachers sometimes strike them at the end of *savasana* as a way of gently bringing you back. But Bolster was confused. He'd been practicing on his own and hadn't been playing any recorded music. The bowl went off again.

Bolster realized that it was his ringtone.

He reached over and grabbed his phone off the coffee table. It was Martinez. Ajoy's memorial service wasn't scheduled to start for another three hours.

"What?" Bolster said.

"I'm in Hollywood," Martinez said.

"So?" said Bolster.

Martinez gave him an address.

"You'd better get down here," he said.

TWENTY

———— o ————

BOLSTER SHOWERED, SHAVED, AND EVEN SPLASHED HIMSELF with scent. He didn't own a suit, but he had a decent sport coat, which he put over a clean collared shirt. A pair of pants that weren't jeans, a reasonably clean pair of black loafers, and a tie, solid black, rounded out the outfit. He didn't look like a magazine model, but he hardly looked like a bum. Every man should have at least one grown-up outfit.

Odds were that he wasn't going to get home before the service. He had to drive from Santa Monica to Hollywood late on a Saturday morning, a heavenly sounding errand to most of the world. But Bolster knew it was purgatory for sure, a dreary slog with no good choices. The 10 to the 110 to the 101? Too much backtracking, and if there was anything going on at the Convention Center, all hope was lost. His secondary-street options weren't much better. He might be able to skirt the worst of the Culver City farmers' market bleed-over, but the only noninsane route would take him through the heart of West Hollywood.

In the end, there was nothing to do but drive.

Forty-five minutes later, Bolster pulled Whitey up just off Western between Sunset and Franklin, in front of an apartment building, a three-story job painted blue and white more than a decade earlier, which somehow looked one-story because the windows were so narrow. A tall, iron-gated garage threatened the street like an angry mouth. It was the building's most prominent feature, and the most advertised on the apartment-rental sites. Off-street parking always allowed the landlord to charge two grand plus, no matter how degraded the building.

There were two cop cars parked in the driveway, plus Martinez's generic detective's Altima. No one was getting into or out of that building for a while. A cop at the entrance eyed Bolster suspiciously.

"Matt Bolster. I'm working with Detective Martinez."

"Hold on," the cop said.

The cop pulled out a smartphone, texted something, and looked up.

"How's it going, man?" Bolster said.

"It's going OK, sir," said the cop tensely.

He needed to do some yoga.

The cop's phone buzzed. He looked down.

"Martinez says you can go up," he said. "Second floor. Number 203."

The door to apartment 203 had been propped open. Bolster entered a virtual shrine to Ajoy Chaterjee. There were photos and posters up everywhere of Ajoy, from all phases of his career: young Ajoy, sleek and beautiful, standing on one hand in the park; cheeky mogul Ajoy, wearing nothing but star-spangled yoga shorts, American flag in one hand and a stuffed eagle on his shoulder; Ajoy on the covers of regional yoga magazines; Ajoy laughing; Ajoy being serious; a poster of the Sequence, Ajoy performing each pose to perfection. There was also a poster of the putatively enlightened jam musician Michael Franti. *Don't look Franti in the eye*, Bolster thought.

The room smelled like stale incense.

Something had gone very wrong in this dusty, yoga prop–strewn den.

Bolster heard voices from an interior room.

"Hello?" he said.

Martinez appeared in the door frame and gestured Bolster forward.

In the bedroom, slumped over a desk, was the body of Greg Vining. Or at least what remained. Half of Vining's head was splattered around the room.

"Oh, man," Bolster said.

"You know him?" Martinez asked.

"Greg Vining. He was part of Ajoy's inner circle of teachers. He's also the guy who hit me in the face with a guitar."

"A neighbor heard the shot," Ajoy said. "When the cops saw all the weird Ajoy stuff, they called me in."

"What do you know so far?"

"Well, it was a handgun."

"Three-day waiting period, obtained four days ago?"

"Exactly. And it looks like Vining did it himself."

"How do you know?"

"The bullet angle matches up. His fingerprints were the only ones on the gun."

"Still."

"There was no sign of forced entry anywhere."

"He could have let someone in."

"The door was bolted when we got here," Martinez said, "including one lock that could only be attached from the inside. And there's no egress point. There doesn't appear to be anything unusual going on."

"Just another run-of-the-mill, Saturday-morning, East Hollywood yoga suicide," Bolster said.

"Exactly," said Martinez.

"You find anything else?"

"There was a note. Of sorts."

"Really."

Martinez produced an evidence bag. He pulled out a piece of computer paper, now encased in a plastic sleeve. On it was written, in red block letters, "IT'S ALL A LIE." The paper also contained a fair splatter of blood and brain matter.

"The shadow side," Bolster said.

"What?" said Martinez.

"Yoga is all about light. But it has a shadow. Vining saw the darkness."

"Seriously, Bolster?"

"Shut up, dude," Bolster said. "I've studied this stuff. You want my help or not?"

"Fine, a shadow," said Martinez.

"Thank you. Anyway, Vining believed in the promise that yoga will always make you feel good. When that promise was taken away from him, he went nuts."

"So you think he killed Ajoy?"

"Probably not," said Bolster. "I met the guy. He didn't have the stones."

Bolster looked around the room. It was mostly band posters in here, and mostly from the '90s. Vining had been a singer-songwriter type, but apparently had never gotten beyond the 9:00 p.m. Tuesday slot at the Silverlake Lounge. The last notice was from 2002, and even that was starting to look yellowed. Bolster guessed that was when Vining had gone down the yoga rabbit hole. You could always, if you knew enough, figure out the time when yoga made the leap from hobby to obsession in someone's life.

"I need a minute," Bolster said.

Martinez cleared the room, even though the other cops protested.

"Did you pull a laptop?" Bolster asked.

"Of course," said Martinez.

"Can I see it?"

Martinez left for a second and then came back with a beaten-down-looking white 2007 MacBook, which, naturally, had an

Ajoy Yoga sticker on the cover. The little white light was still glowing at the base.

"You forgot to turn it off," Bolster said.

"Figured you might have some interest."

Martinez handed Bolster a pair of evidence gloves, which Bolster put on, and then handed over the machine.

It's not like Bolster possessed any kind of special observational skills; in fact, he was pretty lousy at the detail work. There was no way he'd be able to deduce anything by looking closely. His gift was generality; he let his partners handle the microscope. Bolster had a knack for picking up the *vibe* of a situation. And nothing was more vibey than yoga.

That said, Bolster secretly enjoyed snooping on other people's computers. Nothing said more about a modern person than his or her browser history. Bolster sat on Vining's bed, which was both springy *and* mushy. It had been a long time since this guy had invested in a mattress. For all his handsomeness, and all his yoga skills, Greg Vining had clearly been alone in life, and broke. Bolster knew the feeling.

Vining's browser history showed the same signs of Ajoy obsession as his apartment did. Late Friday afternoon, Vining had been watching archival YouTube footage of Ajoy doing yoga in the '80s, including a strange ten-minute scene of him teaching the Sequence to Jane Fonda. There was also something called "Ajoy Yoga–Gangnam Style Mashup," which Bolster avoided but which Vining had apparently watched twice. Toward the top of the column, Bolster saw listings for "Yoga to Heal a Broken Heart," "Ten Poses to Help You with Depression," and a Yelp page for the Pink Elephant liquor store where Charles Bukowski had bought his swill two L.A. generations ago.

Vining's demise had been swift, scary, and sad, representing behavior way beyond ordinary mourning. He'd watched videos of his guru, gotten drunk, and then blown out his brains. *Maybe he did kill Ajoy Chaterjee*, Bolster thought. At the very least, he'd known something.

The memorial service started in an hour. Bolster closed the browser, but before he shut the machine down, he saw an unlabeled .mov file on the laptop screen. On a hunch, he e-mailed it to himself, making a note to watch it later.

He left the room, handed Martinez the computer, and took off his plastic gloves.

"Someone bag that poor guy up," he said.

Greg Vining had been scheduled to play at Ajoy's memorial. It would have been his biggest crowd ever. But he was going to have to skip the gig.

TWENTY-ONE

———— o ————

THE AIR AT AJOY YOGA HEADQUARTERS HAD TURNED QUIET, muted, respectful, and, Matt Bolster thought, a little boring. He and Martinez came through the door a quarter hour before the service. They'd transformed the studio into a funeral parlor with a vaguely Indian bent, decorated with tasteful black bunting and red roses. At the center of the lobby, on the front desk, sat a stunning triptych tapestry depicting the necrotic adventures of Yama, the ancient Hindu god of death. This seriously expensive global treasure was on loan from Ajoy's private collection. His ex-wife, Dottie, had gotten most of the art in their divorce, and Ajoy had barely whimpered. He'd apparently already given up by then.

Ajoy Chaterjee, or at least the classic, pre–psychic unraveling version of him, loved a big show with lots of glitz and flashy dancers. He once spent three months opening up a ten-thousand-square-foot studio in Vegas, when three days clearly would have done the job. But when Ajoy died, his Sequence quickly lost its power. His broke-ass beginning students were already thinking about seeking their next guru, forming the next attachment, taking with them their keening, obnoxious circle drumming and technically flawed public displays of *asana* prowess that had turned the sidewalk around the San Vicente studio into an Occupy-style display of public yoga mourning. Five days on, that was almost over, and Ajoy, or at least the gnarled body and hideously distended tongue that had once been called Ajoy, was living in a frozen drawer at the Santa Monica morgue.

No one was crying at Ajoy Chaterjee's memorial service. The big room at Ajoy Yoga headquarters featured lots of serious-looking faces (and about just as many stunning little black dresses), but it was as dry as the Playa on Labor Day. Bolster scanned the room, seeing a few vaguely recognizable second-tier actors, and also Martha Wickman, who was wearing a black pantsuit and blouse, silver-dotted with spangles, that resembled something midcareer Johnny Cash would have worn. The colors were respectful, but the cut was less than demure. She had powerful arms, sharply defined. They were certainly capable, Bolster thought, of snapping bone.

Martha was whispering something to the guy next to her, who whispered back and made her laugh. *Why,* Bolster wondered, *is no one mourning here?* She spotted Bolster and gave him a wink. He waved her over.

"What's up, Bolster?" she said.

"We need to talk when this is over," he said.

"Why?" she said, a little too loudly. "Because you think I killed Ajoy?"

He motioned for her to keep it down.

"There are a lot of loose ends."

"There are always loose ends, Bolster. Why would I kill my mentor?"

"Cash?"

"Money's not an issue," she said.

"Revenge?"

"For what?"

"Sexual jealousy?"

Now he was just spitballing.

"Nah," Martha said. "I prefer my guys stoned and stubbly."

She smacked Bolster on the ass. He looked around to see if anyone was paying attention. They weren't.

"Look me up when this is over," she said.

He still hadn't ruled her out. In fact, he hadn't ruled anybody out, including Greg Vining, who was also dead. The only person in the room whom he *didn't* suspect was Suzie Hahn, who was smiling and waving at him from a seat in the fourth row.

"Hi, Matt!" she said. "I saved you a seat!"

"Great," Bolster said, trying to smile back.

He didn't really want to sit with Suzie Hahn, but the fourth row was a perfect vantage point for him: close enough to the action to observe everything, but not right on top. Bolster believed in blending. He looked for Martinez, who'd established himself standing near the back door, arms crossed like a surly security guy at a concert. Martinez had no real interest, professional or personal, in the proceedings. He was just there as muscle in case someone went after Bolster, which was a pretty likely scenario, after all.

Bolster had no outs. He went over and sat next to Suzie Hahn.

"*How's it going?*" she asked in a loud whisper.

"It's fine."

"*I mean with the investigation.*"

"I know what you mean, Suzie."

"Well," she said, "I'm glad you're here. I wouldn't have missed it, personally."

"What are you doing here, anyway?" he said. "I thought they weren't allowing press."

"I just batted my eyes," she said, batting her eyes. "If it's yoga, I'm there."

A high-end memorial service like this demanded a sober attitude, but there was still an air of exclusivity, like at any L.A. event. The invitational pecking order spanned the calendar from the Golden Globes to the Yom Kippur breakfast, and the human life cycle from christening to wedding to death. You weren't anyone unless you got invited to the right parties. In some ways, funeral and memorial services were the most rarefied scores of all, because they happened suddenly, and only once. Death was the ultimate velvet rope, and everyone wanted to know what was on the other side. Whom you were invited to say good-bye to in public was the ultimate determination of your social status. And then there were people like Suzie Hahn, regulars in the know who could always talk their way onto the list.

The room buzzed with respectful but still audible chatter, as though everyone were getting ready to see a potential Oscar contender screened for the first time. While Suzie excitedly live-tweeted updates from the scene, Bolster looked around in time to see Marcus Robinson make his grand entrance, accompanied by his wife (a stunning, grand-foreheaded beauty rumored to be descended from Ethiopian royalty), his three children, Magic Johnson, and at least two different producers who worked closely with Will Smith. Once again, Robinson had surrounded himself with a hassle-proof, arrest-proof human shield of L.A.'s black elite. Bolster made sure to give him the thousand-yard stare, and to keep it locked as Robinson made his way down the aisle, glad-handing everyone he came across, the Roman consul enjoying the last days before the barbarians knocked down the gates. Eventually, he saw Bolster, gave a little smile, put his hands together at his chest in *anjali mudra*, and bowed slightly. Bolster gave him the same back, trying his best to imbue this gesture of peace with a tinge of menace.

By the time Robinson and his entourage of family and trusted associates sat down, it was about five minutes after two. Nearly every seat in the place was full, a miracle by L.A. standards, where only industry-sponsored music showcases started on time. Dottie Chaterjee, the widow, appeared in the doorway, resplendent in a white mourning sari, at the head of a phalanx of relatives, several of whom looked on the verge of open weeping.

"Dottie looks sad," Suzie said.

Her face was indeed grim; her mouth turned down sourly. Ajoy had been her husband for decades, had fathered her children, and had paid for her breast augmentation. She had much to mourn. Bolster felt relieved to be seeing what appeared to be an actual display of grief, rather than a ludicrously pseudospiritual New Age pantomime.

Dottie Chaterjee walked down the center aisle, nodding at people politely, but not glad-handing as Marcus Robinson had done. She stopped only once, in front of Bolster's row. When she saw him sitting on the aisle, she said, "Mr. Bolster."

"Ms. Chaterjee?" Bolster replied.

"I have something for you."

From the folds of her sari, Dottie pulled a manila folder thick with paper. She handed it to Bolster.

"You may find this useful for your purposes," she said. Then she walked on, comforting a withered auntie who'd begun to softly sob.

Bolster held the folder, sorely tempted to open it and review the contents, but he realized that this probably wouldn't be the place. But he also had nowhere to stash it, and didn't really want to slide a potential smoking gun under his folding chair. As though she'd read his mind, Suzie took the folder from him and slid it into her bag. She winked.

"I'll give it to you afterward, untouched," she said.

Bolster thanked her. He turned his head. Marcus Robinson was glaring at him.

"Do it quickly," Bolster said.

The room exploded with a loud burst of Indian music. In the doorway stood Chelsea Shell, wearing a black sari and matching black veil, her hair done up like Audrey Hepburn's in the post-conversion scenes of *My Fair Lady*, her forehead streaked with ash. She struck a pose of grief, the left side of her chin tucked into her left shoulder, her eyes downcast, her lashes nearly as long as her shapely, amazing legs. In her right hand, Chelsea Shell held a microphone.

The death show was about to begin.

"I was one of Ajoy's closest students," Chelsea said. "I was supposed to be joined today by Greg Vining, who wrote this song. But he's chosen to grieve privately."

She doesn't know, Bolster thought. *Or does she?*

Whether she knew or not, Chelsea began to shimmy down the aisle.

"Ajoy is love," she breathed into the mic, "and love is Ajoy."

A burst of horrendous music filled the room, that very contemporary sound that's part Vedic devotional, part white suburban hip-hop, but always overwhelmed by New Age harmonium and strings. Chelsea reached the stage and sang.

Ajoy Yoga
Ajoy Yoga
From Manhattan
To Kenosha
Whether Paris
Or in Rome
Ajoy Yoga
Found a home

If I'd written those lyrics, I'd kill myself, too, Bolster thought, realizing right away that was the wrong thing to think. Bolster often found himself wishing for guitars, of the nonacoustic variety, in yoga music, but he knew that was probably a distant dream. Chelsea was delivering a kind of soft-rock version of rap, the current mode in yoga entertainment. Bolster felt embarrassed for her, but he had to admit that she owned the performance with a weird sort of sincerity. She gave a little shake and a little hip-cock and breathed soulfully into the microphone, her shimmering beauty a testament to the effectiveness of her quasi-ayurvedic lifestyle, if not exactly to her full sanity.

Ajoy Chaterjee made the Sequence / And he gave our lives some meaning / All the poses done in order / To knock down our mental borders / Sweat and laughter / Sun and sand / Helping out our fellow man / Ajoy gave it all to us / He was our teacher / Not our boss / And we loved him!

Then came a repeat of the chorus.

Elaborately costumed dancers, both male and female, streamed down the center aisle and also from the room's left and right wings, writhing to faux-Indian instrumental bombast. Even above the music, which was way louder than it should have been, Bolster could hear a few distressed moans from the crowd. In the front row, Dottie Chaterjee was burying her face in her hands as she watched her ex-husband's substantial legacy subsumed by the collective mania of a brainwashed crew of yogic carnival barkers. It would have been bad enough if this were the tribute to a man whose life had run its natural course, but Ajoy had been horribly disfigured and publicly humiliated. He deserved something better, or at least subtler. But still, Chelsea Shell chanted on:

Ajoy Chaterjee gave us yoga / And his yoga made us good / Taught us how to be ourselves / Worked just like he said it would / Sideways plank and downward dog / Alligator, camel, frog / Asana and pranayama / *Good for Papa, good for Mama…*

Even the ever-supportive, relentlessly positive Suzie Hahn, sitting next to Bolster, gasped at that one.

Ajoy Yoga
Ajoy Yoga
From Pasadena
To the ocean
San Francisco
Or L.A.
Ajoy Yoga's
Here to stay

A blast of incomprehensible music followed, accompanied by a brief flurry of Bollywood-style dance moves. A half dozen of the dancers stacked together, one behind the other, moving their arms angularly as though to resemble Lord Shiva himself. On either side of them, one man and one woman dropped in *hanumanasana*, otherwise known as the splits, a pose that no sane person over thirty should ever try, unless he was genetically predisposed. They posed there in this ritualistic tableau, a living testament to everything that was wrong in American yoga culture.

Then the music stopped, mercifully. Bolster assumed that the show was over and the true memorial service could finally begin. But no. The female dancers unfurled their saris. The male ones took off their dress pants and nice shirts. Underneath, they wore skimpy yoga shirts and, for the women, sports bras. They took a formation onstage and stood, ramrod-straight yet somehow at ease; took a collective deep, long, full breath; and began to do the Sequence, one pose at a time.

The students executed the poses perfectly, and in unison. They didn't skip anything, and they didn't rush, either, much to the audience's substantial chagrin. Perfect pelvic alignment, considered carefully, framed their every twist. They contracted their hamstrings in their forward bends and pulled in their perinea when necessary. It was yoga as ritual, and it sucked.

Unless you're the teacher, watching someone else do yoga is like watching someone else praying. It's deeply boring and terribly personal. But everyone had to sit there in that hot room with the stains on the walls and watch as Ajoy Chaterjee's prize hens clucked through their precious Sequence. When done properly, the Sequence took at *least* an hour and ten minutes, maybe more, and that was without *savasana*. Were they really going to torture the crowd for that long?

Fortunately for the collective sanity of the gathered, no one was more frustrated than Dottie Chaterjee. As the surviving members of Ajoy's Circle, plus their friends who stood just outside the Circle, crested into their third consecutive wide-legged forward bend, she stood up regally.

"I have had *enough* of you pathetic yoga monkeys!" Dottie shouted.

The yoga people paused midpose. Dottie waved at them dismissively.

"Shoo!" she said. "Shoo!"

"But..." one of them said, "it's the Sequence."

"No one cares about your Sequence," she said. "Do it on your own time."

Most of the people in the room applauded. Bolster sat still, trying to remain objective, but he certainly approved. Sometimes the human ego needed a stern and unpermissive parent.

Ajoy's showy students slunk off the stage. Chelsea Shell, in particular, looked cowed and ashamed, as though she'd been caught doing something inappropriate in public. She slunk toward the back of the room, wrapping her sari around her, hoping that people would avert their eyes. Bolster looked at her as she walked away. She saw him and gave a burning, tearful look, a mix of guilt and neediness shot through with desire, which caused his stomach to flip. He simultaneously wanted to soothe her and cuss her out. Maybe he'd get the chance to do both later.

Dottie stood in front of the crowd. She spoke calmly and forcefully, a skill honed from decades of chairing fund-raisers.

"I knew Ajoy Chaterjee better than all of you combined," she said. "He probably would have enjoyed that show."

The crowd laughed.

"But do you think that's really how he'd want to be remembered? Ajoy wasn't a showman, or a show-off, or a tycoon"—and with that word, she glared at Marcus Robinson, who was sitting right in front of her. "He was simply a yoga teacher, and even more simply a man. When I met him, a thousand years ago, he was brash and a little flashy, yes, but he was also gentle and patient and, most importantly, lots of fun. He didn't seem overwhelmed by ambition and had no professional goals other than spreading the word about a very good thing to people who needed his help. Even after he got famous—and he got very, very famous—he still stayed somewhat humble. Ajoy spent years living outside, actually in the dirt. He knew that the mansion he'd bought was an illusion. Only toward the end, when something…*else* got hold of him, did he let his ego take control."

Dottie's eyes filled with what appeared to be actual tears. It was hard for the crowd, Bolster included, not to follow.

"I won't deny that the last few years with him were hard," she said. "I kicked his butt out of the house for a reason."

This brought some laughter. Dottie was playing the crowd.

"But I'll always remember Ajoy as a husband, father, lover, and friend. Those weren't roles for him. They were *real*. When he took the stage to teach his Sequence, that was Show Ajoy, which was fine, even necessary. He taught me, as he taught you all, so much. The Sequence may die—at least I hope it does, because that thing is *hard*—but his greater legacy will endure."

People in the audience were applauding, a few were cheering, and many more were now openly weeping. Hollywood loves itself a good cry almost as much as it loves a good performance, and Dottie had performed her role to the hilt. Bolster wasn't sure he bought it, but then again, he wasn't sure if he bought anything anymore. This whole situation felt like a surrealist yoga play put on for his behalf. It got a lot more surreal when the applause died.

"It's important that the world remembers Ajoy as he really was," Dottie said. "The truth is important. Especially when it comes to his substantial business interests."

Oh boy, Bolster thought.

Dottie looked straight at Marcus Robinson, whose face was plastered with an implacable smile that said, *Do not fuck with me, woman.*

"The fact is," Dottie continued, "after we divorced, Ajoy was short on money. Mostly because I had really good lawyers. His were good, too. But mine were better."

Some snickers drifted around the room, but not many. Bolster got the sense that things were about to get *really* uncomfortable. Next to him, Suzie Hahn sat on the edge of her seat, looking very excited. All she needed was a bucket of popcorn. Martinez stood by the back door, arms crossed, looking bored as usual.

"Ajoy and his partners made some risky investments, like all businesspeople do. Not all of them worked, and the great Ajoy enterprise lost money. But there were also dummy corporations, fake bank accounts, slush funds, and all kinds of other strangeness a little too complicated for my tastes. The teacher pension fund that Ajoy spent years accumulating? It's gone. Most of the mortgages on the studios that Ajoy actually owned are either in default or heading there. All production of Ajoy-related merchandise has ceased. And here's the thing: it was all going to happen whether Ajoy died or not. His business partners made sure of that."

The people in the room murmured nervously. Next to Bolster, Suzie Hahn took furious notes, the line between scene blogger and serious reporter now erased by the exclusive scoop of a lifetime. Marcus Robinson stood up.

"She has no real evidence," he said. "Ajoy Yoga is alive and well, and it will be for the foreseeable future."

"I do have evidence, Marcus," Dottie said. "Dozens and dozens of photocopied pages' worth of evidence."

Suzie clutched at her shoulder bag and gave Bolster a look.

"It's in the hands of investigators," she continued, "who are ready to make an arrest." Her eyes turned to the fourth row, where Bolster and Suzie Hahn sat.

Don't look at me, thought Bolster. *I'm a private contractor.* He couldn't arrest anybody.

"On what charge?" asked Marcus Robinson.

"Ajoy was going to expose you," Dottie says. "I'd say conspiracy to commit murder."

"I didn't murder *anyone*," Marcus Robinson shouted. "That's not how we do business."

Bolster could almost hear Martinez sigh from the back. If this were all true, it meant Magic Johnson was involved, however indirectly, and that meant Martinez would have to talk to the cameras, which he hated to do. Still, he came down the aisle, ready to do his job. Bolster and Suzie, who were, after all, in possession of the precious documents, stood as well, and passed Martinez on the way to the exit. Magic and the higher-placed movie producers got up and stood to the side, looking nonchalant, as if to say, *This is not our deal.* Marcus Robinson was going to run out of friends quickly.

Apparently, he was going to run out of the room as well. Two of his larger thugs got up with him. They charged Martinez like angry rhinos, knocking him to the ground. Robinson followed behind them, smooth and athletic.

"Ooh," Suzie said to Bolster. "This is so *exciting*!"

"I'm used to it," Bolster said.

Martinez got up quickly but looked winded. The situation was quickly devolving into a seat-snapping panic, just short of someone yelling, "Fire!" in a crowded yoga studio. Robinson's rhino-men kept charging, right toward Bolster and Suzie.

"I hope you can run," Bolster said.

"I can do everything," Suzie said.

Bolster didn't doubt her.

They raced out of the studio, into the lobby and past the desk where Casey Anderson sat, obliviously, with his earbuds in. Robinson's thugs were maybe thirty steps behind them, with Robinson trailing a little, striding strong. Martinez served as a kind of wheezing caboose to this chase-train. He was probably the only one among them who didn't do yoga.

On the street, the sun hit Bolster's eyes with a scream. The day was brighter than an after-school program for indigo children. Bolster made a snap decision to turn left on San Vicente, and an even snappier decision to never do anything that even tangentially involved Marcus Robinson again. He had some stamina, but this was making him very tired.

Suzie kept up with him, though her strides were short. She smiled happily, like she was a puppy turned loose in an enclosed run. They headed southeast, toward Crenshaw and the furniture stores and gas stations, where three enormous black men chasing a white dude and a Korean American woman while being chased themselves by an out-of-shape Mexican cop wouldn't seem quite as strange. If they'd turned toward Beverly Hills, it would have been on YouTube within ten minutes.

On their right, across the street, there was nothing but retail, much of it poorly trafficked and most of it shuttered, save a couple of medical-marijuana shops that Bolster knew, from consumer experience, were little more than fronts for the Russian Mob—an unfortunate side effect of the form that California's medical-marijuana boom had taken on the always-untrustworthy streets of L.A. But now wasn't the time to ponder the ethics of pot retail. Bolster and Suzie appeared to be losing ground, although not as badly as Martinez, who was now almost a full city block behind Robinson. To his credit, he hadn't quit yet.

Still, this couldn't go on for long. Suzie clutched her shoulder bag tightly by her side. She held the documents that would bring down the Ajoy Yoga empire. If they survived the afternoon, Bolster would make copies for her. This would be the scoop that exploded her traffic. She might even make a little ad money or get some paid gigs out of the deal. Blogging really had triumphed over old media.

"I have an idea," she said.

Bolster wasn't sure he wanted to put his life in the hands of Suzie Hahn's whims, but that was more than he could say.

"Follow me," she said.

They turned a corner onto a side street, which was dominated on the left by an enormous self-storage depot. Suzie jogged through the entry gate, winking at the security guard. He winked back at her.

"You know everyone, don't you?" Bolster said.

"Only the important people," Suzie replied.

They had maybe thirty seconds before Robinson's thugs caught them, perhaps a little more if the security guard got in their way. The storage center was nothing but a concrete tunnel surrounded by a ten-foot wall topped with barbed wire, and more than one hundred metal doors, but Suzie seemed to know where she was jogging.

A few units down, she stopped at a door, reached down, and pulled it open.

"We're going to hide in a storage unit?" Bolster asked.

"This one is specialized," Suzie said.

Bolster beheld *zazen*. Comfortable pillows patterned with red, orange, and gold were scattered throughout the unit. There were a half dozen people sitting, backs against the wall, legs crossed, faces looking serene. The unit smelled like sandalwood incense. A low hum filled the space, and a statue of the Buddha, surrounded by the candles, sat in the back corner on a small wooden table. Up front, holding the space, was Lora Powell, Bolster's meditation teacher. She looked up, gently put a finger to her lips, and motioned for Bolster and Suzie to sit down. Suzie quickly pulled shut the steel door to the unit so Robinson's guys couldn't find them. She typed something into her phone and showed it to Bolster.

"*It's a secret meditation club,*" said the screen.

Of course it is, he thought.

Bolster was sweaty and his heart was beating way too fast. Plus, he had thirst. This wasn't an optimal situation for meditating. On the other hand, it provided a handy escape to a potentially deadly problem. He looked at Lora, stuck out his tongue, and put his hands to his throat. She nodded and gestured him forward, pulling a BPA-free water bottle out of her bag. He took it gladly and chugged, even though she'd treated the water with some sort of vitamin-rich nutrition powder. It went down sour but probably reduced his chances of catching a cold that day by 30 percent.

Suzie was already on her meditation pillow, legs crossed into lotus, forearms resting on her knees, thumbs and forefingers pressed together, forming an O shape. The masters call this the "seal of wisdom." *How can she transition so fast?* Bolster thought. His heart hammered. On the verge of finally locking this murder down, now he was supposed to sit quietly for a while? Gandhi once said, "I am so busy, I shall have to meditate twice as long." Matt Bolster was no Gandhi, but he didn't really have a choice.

So Bolster sat, crossing his legs in the regular way because his knees started to hurt if he went into *padmasana* for too long, and he breathed, counting his inhales, letting them become longer and fuller, observing the racetrack of his mind, absorbing the sounds and smells around him, going inside as the world outside bumbled along, panicking, fermenting, making plans that would never be actualized, churning in all its beautiful, horrible, idiotic splendor. He had the here and now in this dark, safe, weird storage space.

A gong sounded. Bolster looked at his phone. It had been half an hour. Suzie Hahn looked at him and winked. She walked over to the door and opened it a crack. Then a little more. It was like staring into a searchlight, but Bolster felt oddly calm.

Martinez was leaning against the hood of a cop car, writing on a pad.

"Catching up on your paperwork?" Bolster asked.

"There you are," Martinez said. "What the hell were you doing in a storage unit?"

"Meditating," Bolster said.

"Fucking hippie," said Martinez. "We caught Marcus Robinson and his two guys. Charged him with Ajoy's murder, though he says he didn't do it. We're taking him downtown for processing anyway."

"That seems like a safe bet," Bolster said.

"Come by on Monday and I'll write you a check."

"OK."

"And we'll need those papers."

"I'm gonna let Suzie make copies first," Bolster said. "She kept them safe."

"Fair enough."

Suzie appeared in the light, squinting.

"You've got yourself a story," Bolster said.

———— o ————

It was dusk by the time Bolster got into Whitey to head home. He had a text from Chelsea Shell. *I need to see u*, it said. Seeing Chelsea was something he both wanted and didn't want, like when you haven't eaten in a while and you pass by a burger joint and you know you'd be better off eating something else, anything else, really, or even not eating at all and waiting until the morning to save your gut the grief, but you're burger hungry and there's no way to really resist. When it came to Chelsea Shell, Bolster was always burger hungry.

Meet me at home in 30, he texted back.

He'd been in his apartment for five minutes, barely enough time to plop down half a can of wet salmon for Charlemagne, when she knocked at his door. She was still wearing the outfit from the memorial service. Makeup had streaked her face where she'd been crying. She threw her arms around Bolster, and he hugged back, wondering if grief sex was just around the corner.

"Greg Vining is dead," she said.

"I know," said Bolster. "I saw the body at the scene."

"Why didn't you tell me?"

"I didn't have a chance. You were too busy showing off your awesome dance moves."

"That was probably a mistake."

"You think?"

"Poor Greg," Chelsea said. "Ajoy was his life."

"And his—"

"Don't say it," Chelsea said.

"OK," said Bolster. "You want a beer?"

"Oh my God, *yes*," Chelsea said.

She came in and sprawled on his couch. He popped her a cold one, and one for himself.

"I'll join you in a second," Bolster said. "I've just got to make an Internet run."

He went onto Suzie Hahn's site. Some of the financials were already up, but she was breaking the news slowly to maximize traffic, holding back some of the juiciest stuff for the Monday-morning news cycle, when the real blogs would pick it up. Soon the world would know: Ajoy Yoga, thanks to Marcus Robinson, had essentially been turned into a dummy corporation, complete with its own offshore bank accounts and overleveraged investments in other companies that didn't even have a chance. Why had Robinson killed Ajoy, though? Had Ajoy had second thoughts, or had he been threatened into blowing the whistle when he found out what was really happening to his life's work? That would all come out in court.

"You've got to look at this," Bolster said.

Chelsea got up to examine the evidence.

"That's crazy," she said. "I had no idea."

Bolster went over to his e-mail and saw the .mov file he'd sent himself from Greg Vining's computer earlier in the day. He'd almost totally forgotten about it. He downloaded it and, without thinking, clicked Play.

The footage was somewhat dark and grainy, but still clear enough. It was Ajoy Yoga's headquarters, and it looked like night. A dark, evil-sounding chant played in the background. *Ommmmmmmm…Ommmmmmmmmmm…Ah-ommmm mmmmmm*, it went, in a loop, sounding like the call to dinner in hell. Ajoy's private "throne" sat in plain view, dead center, starkly lit by bright-red floodlights. Around the throne, Bolster could make out a half dozen people, maybe as many as eight. They were sitting on pillows in the relative darkness.

As the music played, Ajoy Chaterjee mounted the throne. He sat down facing the people on the pillows. Bolster wasn't sure how, but Ajoy's eyes were opened freakishly wide, almost like he'd glued open the lids. That had to hurt. In his left hand, Ajoy held a razor blade, of the old-fashioned, straight-razor variety. He opened his mouth very wide, curled up his tongue, and raised his hand. He was going to cut.

"Oh," said Chelsea Shell. "Oh, no."

EPISODE 6

TWENTY-TWO

———— o ————

A JOY PUT THE RAZOR BLADE DOWN ON THE ARM OF HIS throne. Relief moved through Bolster like a full-body wash, though he wasn't quite sure why. It wasn't as though the file was going to reveal some alternate reality where Ajoy didn't die. Bolster knew how this movie ended. So, apparently, did Chelsea Shell, who was turning sideways, barely looking at the screen, withering into herself.

"Please turn it off," she said. "I can't see this again."

Bolster paused the file.

"What do you mean, *again*?" said Bolster. "You were in the room?"

"I was," she said. "We all were, the whole Circle. Ajoy had sent us a group text message two hours before and said it was urgent. That he had something for us that would reveal the true secrets of yoga."

"But I thought you were done with him."

"Dearest Matt," she said sadly. "He was still our guru."

He looked at her with equal parts lust and pity.

"Did you kill him?" he asked.

"No, honey," she said. "But I'm still guilty."

"What do you mean?"

Chelsea took a deep breath, using her best technique.

"Just watch," she said. "I'll sit here, too. It's my punishment. I deserve it."

Matt started the video again. The long, deep *ohmmmmm* sound continued to play in the background like a summons to hell. Ajoy reached behind him and pulled out a few sheaths of paper, which looked worn, like they'd been read many times.

"I hold in my hand," Ajoy said, "the original words of the *Anihatra Kura*, the holiest of all ancient yogic purifying rituals. It has been passed down, in secret, from guru to student throughout the eons. And now I'm going to present it to you."

He explained: "When the Vedic priests discovered yoga, in the early days, it gave them almost unlimited power. They could levitate, they could hypnotize people, and they could stop time. Some of them lived for hundreds of years, accumulating great wealth and power, thousands of acres of land. They were great lords of yoga, which turned them into something like charismatic gods.

"But there was also another path," Ajoy continued, "the path of true transcendence. Other yogis did it differently. They could still extend their lives, far beyond what anyone thought possible. But they did so quietly, without a big public show. In the morning, after some ablutions, they would sit on their cushions and begin to inhale, very slowly, as though they were breathing through the stem of a flower. Because of this inhale, the breath moved through their bodies with great subtlety, for a long time, minutes, even hours. The true masters could get through the entire day with only three or four breaths. This required great concentration and patience, and endless practice. They wanted nothing more than to sit and to feel the world pulsate around them. The simple act of breathing, the only thing that all living beings share, filled the darkness of their hearts with the all-seeing light of pure awareness. They experienced reality in its true nature.

"These gurus had few followers. Some of them had none. They offered a difficult way to transcendence, and most people like things to be easy. It was very frustrating, because they knew they were walking the right path. But the other gurus, the wealthy ones, had thousands of followers, even millions. When it was announced they were going to speak, people would crowd into fields, fill great outdoor arenas, just to catch a word of wisdom. And such words these gurus would spill! They'd talk for hours, making their audiences laugh and weep and quiver with joy. It was supreme entertainment, and it required very little effort for the audiences, who left having learned nothing, having done nothing, and having gained nothing of importance. But their gurus just grew wealthier and more powerful. Yoga, as it turned out, was a profitable business."

It was a riveting performance. Bolster could see why an empire had built up around Ajoy Chaterjee. The man possessed unusual charisma. Ajoy continued, on the video:

"The other yogis, the pure ones, knew that something had to be done to stop the corruption of their discipline, which they knew was the most beautiful thing ever devised by humans. They meditated for weeks to make sure they weren't motivated by envy, that most destructive of human emotions. Some of them felt jealous of the famous gurus and retreated to further refine their practices. But others *were* ready. They emerged feeling certain, and were ready to save pure yoga from its usurpers.

"High into the Himalayas they went, to a secret retreat composed of simple huts built around a lake whose sparkling cold waters came from mountain snowmelt. It had the clearest water in the world, so clear that you could see into the future if you looked into it long enough. Personally, I'm skeptical of that claim."

Ajoy gave a little laugh, and so, on the other side of the screen, did Bolster, involuntarily. Of all the details in the story, *this* was the only one that made Ajoy skeptical? It was obvious to Bolster that the whole thing was a myth. Then again, yoga could make seemingly rational people believe all kinds of stupid crap, which was why half the yoga teachers in Santa Monica had shrines to Hanuman in their homes and held monthly Friday-night "Shiva dances" at whatever studio they'd conned into housing their nascent body cult. That served only to prove the central thesis of this video, Ajoy's last lecture. Yoga is very powerful. When the wrong people use that power improperly, it can also be deadly.

Bolster looked behind him. Chelsea had grown paler. The truth seemed to be getting close. On the video, Ajoy continued his story.

A sort of war developed, Ajoy explained. But because it was a yoga war, no shots were fired, no knives unsheathed. The early yogis fought with their minds; their bodies were merely tools in the mental struggle. They began to experiment with rituals, some quite austere, some quite gentle. Early experiments gradually led to more refined practices. It took them many years, but because of the sophistication of their routines and their extended life spans, they had plenty of time. This process, slow and precise like the best science, gave birth to the *Anihatra Kura*, the greatest yogic test of them all.

One by one, the Vedic priests attempted the *Anihatra Kura*. Those who passed retreated to breathe and contemplate further instructions, while those who failed were allowed an indefinite period of recuperation before trying again. The ultimate peace of mind awaited them at the end. Once you scaled the *Kura*'s gates, it was said, you could see through reality itself, and your heart filled with warmth, kindness, and compassion for all living things. *Kura Yoga*, the one true yoga, was born.

It came time to convert the false gurus. The priests left their mountain hideaway and went back into the noisy madness of the secular world, walking with the serene confidence of those who have been through the fire. The false gurus were supremely powerful, though. They lived behind great walls and were protected by unctuous assistants and massive, cruel bodyguards. Reaching them required great trickery on the part of the *Kura* priests.

One of them deployed yoga as a powerful martial art, striking down the bodyguards where they stood, forcing his way into the inner sanctum, where he found the false guru having his sexual way with several acolytes. Others used flattery to gain access to court, while still others disguised themselves as beggars, merchants, disciples, and even, in the case of one diminutive priest who'd developed the *siddhi* to shape-shift his face, a child. Once access was gained, though, they revealed their true selves, presenting the *Anihatra Kura* as a challenge to the false gurus. Only real yogis could pass, they said. A few of the false gurus, sensing a challenge to their supremacy, couldn't be swayed. They reacted violently, exiling the incursive priests and returning to their lives of boundless hedonism and cultish behavior. But most of them retained a shred of humanity from before the time when the great yogic powers had corrupted their souls. They agreed to take the test.

A great many succumbed early, weeping and broken, and instantly abdicated from their heights. Word of this failure spread to their followers. They lost status, and were reduced almost instantly to ordinary men, returning humbled to the streets. Others pushed on, enduring the entire *Kura*. But in the end, they also succumbed, dying where they sat. Their people mourned and occasionally beatified them, but eventually they were forgotten to history, as are we all.

However, a surprising number cleared their *Kura* tests, emerging on the other side into the full flower of enlightenment. Their egos had corrupted them during their period of rule, but not fully. The priests welcomed them into their brotherhood, and the newly converted, in turn, set their followers free onto the world to preach a message of kindness and human compassion, asking them to release themselves from their material attachments, to cut loose their negative emotions, and to love all men and women as their sisters and brothers. This was the final gift of the *Anihatra Kura*, and the great legacy of the original yogis.

"Heavy," Bolster said.

"Just wait," said Chelsea Shell.

On the video, Ajoy said, "I came to this country with the best of intentions and a spirit of joy in my heart, but as the years progressed, I became corrupted by avarice, and lust, and gluttony. I forgot to love those who loved me, and pretended to love others to fulfill my own selfish desires. My original lessons got lost in a sea of hype and ego, and I committed the worst of all possible sins that a yogi can: I gave false teachings. For that, I'm very sorry. But repentance cannot be enough. I built my cult, and it must be taken down."

Next to Bolster, Chelsea started to sob.

"Now," said Ajoy Chaterjee, "the time has come for me to go through my own *Kura*."

TWENTY-THREE

———— o ————

A JOY RAISED HIS LEFT LEG, BRINGING IT UP TO WAIST HEIGHT, cradling his ankle in one hand and his knee in the other. He then rotated it outward at the hip and, very gently, brought it upward so that his foot was parallel with his left ear. Then he tucked his foot behind, nudging it gradually rightward, pushing it so the calf was touching the base of his neck. He kept pushing, ever so carefully, so that the crook of his knee now looked like it supported his head; his foot dangled over his right shoulder like an ungainly earring. This must have been difficult for a man in his sixties to accomplish, even if that man was Ajoy Chaterjee, an undisputed master, but it was also in the realm of yogic possibility. Bolster couldn't do it himself—he'd always be stiff in the hip from the time when a perp had opened a car door on him during a street chase—but he'd certainly seen it done before. What came next, though, was new.

"In the *Anihatra Kura*," Ajoy said, "you must learn to endure pain. Your mind must understand that your body is temporary, and therefore limitless."

That was all wrong, Bolster thought. Yes, your body is temporary, but learning and honoring its limits, which only grow as you age, is all part of the sweet agony of being human. Anything else is torture.

Ajoy reached his left hand down and nudged up his hip slightly. His mouth tightened and his eyes narrowed. Clearly, he'd reached what yoga teachers call "the edge," but he kept pushing. Bolster could almost feel the tendons straining. With a huge push, Ajoy moved his hip up, and Bolster actually heard the pop as his hip went out of joint.

"Ohhhhhhhh," Ajoy said, and not with pleasure. Then he hissed. His temples began to drip sweat. Pain had paid a visit.

"I have begun my *Kura*," he said.

Bolster looked back at Chelsea, who was just short of sucking her thumb at this point.

For the next half hour, Bolster stared in horror at the most sickening display of self-mutilation he'd ever seen. What Ajoy did to himself made any ritual cutting, branding, piercing, coal walking, digestive-cloth passing, or back-alley tattooing look like a trip to the corner store. After popping his left hip out of its socket, he did the same thing to his left knee, bending it down behind his back until it looked like it was just hanging by a few ligaments. Bolster could tell that Ajoy was winging it, almost, as he kept referring to the pages of his *Anihatra Kura* every couple of minutes. Even though his Circle was gasping, unseen, just out of the range of the screen, Ajoy reassured them gently that all would be well, that he would pass through this trial and emerge fulfilled. Bolster was amazed and horrified, because even if Ajoy had survived, which he most definitely had not, it would have taken him years to heal from such injuries. At his age, he would probably never have recovered.

Ajoy's arms were still good, though, so he began to do the same thing to his right leg. *Oh, please don't*, Bolster thought, but there was no way to stop the past from happening again. Then Ajoy, a little more quickly this time, was inching his right foot behind his ear, and then rotating his hip out of the socket, and then, for good measure, wrenching his right ankle back before severing his right knee from its moorings. By now, Ajoy had started crying a little, but he kept breathing and tried to stay brave as he swung his left arm upward through the space between his now-shattered left leg and his torso, landing his left hand just below the shoulder blade. He reached his right hand behind his back, clasped the two hands together, and took a deep breath. With a grunt, he pulled the left hand as hard as he could with the right, until it gave a little bit. Then he pulled again. On the third pull, the shoulder popped. Ajoy shrieked like the dying animal he was.

With another yank, Ajoy dislocated his wrist.

From offscreen, Bolster heard, "Ajoy, stop! Please!"

Ajoy was covered in sweat, but he looked out at his audience and said, quietly, "All is well."

Bolster heard: "No! All is *not* well!"

One of the Circle came up on stage, as if to soothe Ajoy. Or maybe she wanted to get him down from the throne before it was too late. Ajoy waved her off with his one good hand. He was trying to persuade his followers that he'd be fine, when he clearly would not be fine at all.

"Please," he said. "Don't try to stop me. Don't call or e-mail or text anyone. Let me finish. I must do this."

The follower stood down reluctantly. Then, somehow, the great master managed to twist his right arm through just like he had with to his left one. With just will alone (and maybe, Bolster thought mordantly, with a subtle contraction of the *bandhas*), he wrenched that arm out of its socket as well, with a noise that sounded like a drain unstopping. Bolster had no idea how Ajoy endured.

Ajoy moaned slightly and then perched there on his sit bones, like an old doll all torn up and discarded. His breathing grew sad and labored. Light sobs came from the audience. Finally, after a minute or so, Ajoy spoke, his voice now almost desperately soft and humble.

"You may think that I'm feeling pain now," he said. "And I am. It is worse than I thought it would be. My body is broken.

But the *Anihatra Kura* tells us that we must shatter the body to heal the ravaged soul. When the ritual is performed correctly, the body heals itself, more quickly than you could imagine."

"*That is a lie!*" someone shouted, out of camera range.

"No," said Ajoy, "it is not. The purpose of life is to learn that the body is temporary. By destroying it through ritual, we can free ourselves."

Talk about learning the wrong lesson, Bolster thought.

Even uttering those few sentences had made Ajoy tired. His neck slumped. All was silent save that creepy *ah-ommmmmm mmmmm* sound that kept playing over the PA in an endless loop. After a bit, Ajoy lifted his head again.

"But the ritual," he said, "is not yet complete."

Bolster's gut hitched.

"One of the most sacred and ancient yogic practices is the cutting of the frenulum linguae, the little fold of skin that connects the tongue to the base of the mouth. The legends say that when you do that, you can roll your tongue back up into the throat so it can capture the nectar that drips down from your crown chakra once you reach enlightenment. You cut the frenulum a little bit at a time, using an edge of paper or something equally sharp and thin. I don't have time for that, which is why you see the razor blade on the edge of my chair here.

"I need," Ajoy continued, "for one of you to cut my frenulum for me, straight through, in one motion."

Bolster looked back at Chelsea, who'd almost gone catatonic by now. He had little desire to see what came next, but he'd started the case and he was going to see it through to the end.

"*It wasn't me*," Chelsea rasped.

On the video, Ajoy said quietly, "I need a volunteer."

No volunteers presented themselves.

"You are my students," Ajoy said. "You can't leave me like this."

Still no one rose.

"I am *instructing* you to help me," he said.

And yet, nothing.

"*Please.*"

Now the tears came, as the world's most successful yoga teacher found himself begging acolytes to volunteer to cut open his tongue. Behind Bolster, Chelsea was crying. Bolster found himself crying, and he never cried, except at the end of *The Shawshank Redemption.* Everyone in the video was crying, too, including Ajoy himself.

"Don't leave me like this, my friends," he said.

A man walked toward Ajoy. When he reached the throne, he turned around. It was Greg Vining.

"I'll do it, Ajoy," he said.

"Greg," Ajoy said. "You were always my most dependable."

With a nod to his left, Ajoy indicated the razor.

"You must cut it quickly," Ajoy said. "In one motion. Don't extend the process."

Vining's eyes filled with tears. He picked up the razor.

"Finish my *Kura*," Ajoy said.

"Don't do it, Greg!" someone shouted, but Greg was clearly going to do it.

Ajoy opened his mouth wide, sticking his tongue out, drawing it back, and curling it toward the roof, exposing the frenulum. Vining pulled back the razor slightly, moving forward, and with a quick motion cut the linguae clean, like he was snipping fat off a slice of pastrami. Ajoy gave a little squeal and clamped his lips shut over his distended tongue, which hung loose now. With his eyes wide, he looked cartoonish and idiotic.

When Ajoy opened his mouth, blood gushed out like a dam had burst. He screamed horribly, though because his tongue had lost its moorings, the scream had no vibration. It was an agonized death-echo from deep in the back of his palate. The great one met his end, eyes popping, blood pouring, tongue flapping wildly, and his best students all screaming as they watched. Ajoy twitched but couldn't move; he couldn't raise a hand to stanch the blood, and couldn't even begin to walk to the emergency room. Death would reach him soon, but Ajoy had no recognition of his fate. His eyes just registered pain, and nothing else. Greg Vining had wielded the final knife, but, in the balance, Ajoy had slaughtered himself.

Bolster had seen enough. He closed his laptop.

"How could you?" he said to Chelsea.

"How could I *what*?" she said.

"Let him do that. My God."

"We didn't know what it was."

"Oh, come on. You're a smart woman, Chelsea. You could have stopped this shit."

"We *trusted* him, Matt. We thought he knew what he was doing."

"Well, you were wrong."

"Obviously."

Suddenly, Chelsea Shell didn't look so appealing to Bolster anymore. She was just another weak-willed yoga groupie who, in a moment of severe crisis, had been unable to act.

Chelsea stood up.

"I could use a hug," she said.

Bolster stood and embraced Chelsea hard, more to steady himself than out of any real affection or sympathy for her. She stayed in his arms for at least a minute, humming softly, and then pulled up.

"How about a kiss, too?" she said.

"Ask the Circle for one," Bolster said.

They unclenched. Chelsea Shell walked over to the couch and took a big slug of beer.

"I could be something for you, Bolster," she said.

"You're not what I want," he said.

Matt Bolster had let himself become attached, and that attachment had gotten in his way. He nodded toward the door.

Chelsea looked at him sadly and then walked out of his life for good. Bolster didn't worry about her. She'd dine on a steady diet of men for years.

———————— o ————————

After this day, one of the longest in his recent memory, Bolster needed a little personal time. He sat on his couch, smoking a joint. Next to him, his cat, Charlemagne, inhaled passively while watching an insect documentary. Bolster ruminated. Sri Charan Jindra, Ajoy Chaterjee's *own* guru, had expressed severe disappointment in the materialistic turn that yoga had taken in the West. It was a legitimate criticism, but Sri Charan was cruel about it, which left an insecure Ajoy to determine what to do next. Unfortunately, he'd taken the words of some ancient Tantric ritual *way* too seriously. Ajoy had missed the lesson in historical context. He'd done a practice that made no sense in modern times; the Aztecs used to sacrifice virgins to Quetzalcoatl, but that wasn't happening in Mexico City anymore either. Of all the things Ajoy had to pick, why had he chosen the *Anihatra Kura*, the most brutal of all yogic rituals? Sometimes you need to discard the old.

Then again, Bolster thought, he'd never heard of the *Kura* before. What if Ajoy had misinterpreted its meaning? That would make his death even more tragic. He needed to learn more.

Bolster was too stoned to stand by this point, but he managed to lean over the couch and grab his computer off his desk. He couldn't walk, but he could definitely browse. Typing *Anihatra Kura* into Google, he started looking. There were no mentions anywhere, as far as he could see. That wasn't so surprising, really. Obscure yoga terms weren't in huge search-engine demand, and sometimes they got missed or buried. Bolster knew where to go. He had a couple of sites that he checked out from time to time, places that gathered papers that would otherwise have been gathering dust. That's where obscure yoga rituals went to die online. But these places didn't carry a mention either.

He looked for at least an hour, maybe more, but it must have been late when he was done, because the traffic had gone quiet outside. Had he not looked properly, or missed something? A half hour passed without thought. Bolster picked his head up off his chest. He needed to go to bed.

Nine hours later, Bolster woke up, not feeling like complete shit. After drinking two cups of tea, smoking a bowl of Orange Blossom Special, and spending ten minutes in *supta virasana* just to clear the stiffness out of his sacrum, he texted his old friend and sometimes teacher Alan Pastor, professor of Vedic studies at the University of California, Santa Barbara. Alan had forgotten more about yoga history and philosophy than was known to all the teachers ever employed by YogaWorks combined. If anyone had a clue about this *Anihatra Kura*, it was he.

"It's Bolster," Bolster wrote.

Two minutes passed, and then Alan wrote back.

"What's up Bolster?" he replied. "Are u stoned?"

"Of course. I need 2 know some information."

"Go ahead."

"Have u heard of this ancient yoga text called the *Anihatra Kura*?"

A minute passed, and then Alan texted back:

"There is no such animal."

"Are u sure?"

"Not 100% but I've never heard of it and I've heard of everything."

"No literature? It's a ritual."

Another minute passed, this time because Alan was typing a long answer that took two messages to deliver.

"I focus on ancient Vedic and also medieval Tantric, which were the two biggest periods of yoga literature, other than right now. There's never been a mention of an *Anihatra Kura*. Also, translated from Sanskrit, it means 'clean feet.'"

"OK, man," Bolster wrote.

"Smoke one for me," Alan replied.

"I will."

If the *Anihatra Kura* was a ritual about anything, then it was foot washing. But it wasn't, Bolster was pretty sure. Ajoy Chaterjee had been victimized by a horrific joke.

The *Anihatra Kura* didn't exist.

TWENTY-FOUR

───────── o ─────────

Monday morning, Bolster drove Whitey to police headquarters, where Martinez kept a suspiciously paper-free desk. Martinez sat there eating a green chile–chicken tamale and looking unworried about the world.

"I was hoping to never see you again," Martinez said.

"No such luck," said Bolster.

"Why are you interrupting my breakfast?"

"Because you've got to let Marcus Robinson go."

"I don't want to hear that."

The Ajoy killing threatened to tear apart the town, and would probably get Martinez promoted. Everyone had been calling, and all the networks would be carrying the 11 a.m. press conference live, followed by updates on Robinson's sentencing. The Sunday *Times* had blared: "Millionaire Investor Held in Yoga Guru's Death." Plaschke had blathered on in the sports section about the possibility that Magic Johnson was an accessory to murder.

"Well, sorry," Bolster said, "but I've got solid evidence."

He pulled out his phone and called up e-mail. Before leaving the house, Bolster had e-mailed himself the video again. Now he forwarded it on to Martinez.

"I'm sending you something," Bolster said, "that you need to watch alone. And don't let anyone else see it except maybe a judge and Robinson's lawyers. If this went viral, it would do a lot of harm."

"So what is it?"

Bolster leaned in, speaking quietly.

"A video of Ajoy Chaterjee accidentally committing suicide."

"How does someone *accidentally* commit suicide?"

"You'll see," Bolster said. "But you might want to watch on an empty stomach. Which, given that tamale you just horked down, means you're already too late."

"Ajoy didn't have *any* help?" Martinez said. "How is that possible? You saw how his body was broken."

"Anything's possible in yoga."

"Cut it out, Bolster."

"OK, he did have a little help. Greg Vining finished the job for him. You can either declare it a suicide or say that Vining did it. Either way, the killer is dead. Marcus Robinson may face a thousand charges from the SEC, but you can't hold him on a murder rap anymore."

Martinez disappeared for about half an hour to go watch the video in the evidence room. Bolster got a candy bar from the vending machine and waited. When Martinez returned, he looked pale.

"That is some sick shit," he said.

"I know," Bolster said.

"Who thought up that *Kura*?"

"No one did," Bolster said. "It's a hoax."

"What?"

"It's made up, totally."

"How do you know?"

"I know. In any case, when you talk about this to the press, maybe don't mention the *Anihatra Kura*. Just say that Ajoy Chaterjee was killed in a ritual suicide. Or homicide, or suicide combined with homicide. I don't really care—whatever works best for you politically."

"That's fine, Bolster, but who perpetrated the hoax?"

"I've got an idea," Bolster said, "but you'll need to pay me right away."

"Why?"

Bolster wanted to play it casual with Martinez. It was left over from his days as a police; he preferred not to show any emotional connection to the case. Weakness could be perceived as, well, weakness, and Bolster wanted to keep getting work. He'd tossed aside the macho codes the day he quit, but they ran through his bloodstream nonetheless. Still, even though this thing had been solved, he found it gnawing at him. Something very wrong had happened to Ajoy Chaterjee, and that thing sprang from a rot at yoga's heart. This went a lot further than a couple of dead yoga teachers. Ajoy had been a rude jerk to the people around him, particularly toward the end, but his end still needed a full accounting, and Bolster was going to give it to him. Like the Buddha under the Bodhi tree, Matt Bolster wanted to sit down firmly and face the demon, without fear.

"Loose ends," he said.

Bolster deposited the LAPD check before lunchtime. It gave him more money in the bank than at any other time in his life, including the day he quit the force and cashed in his pension. In this town, he knew, that amount of money would barely last a year. But for now he felt pretty flush.

He'd skipped the press conference where Martinez had announced Ajoy's suicide to the public. As Bolster had advised, Martinez omitted any details about what happened and didn't mention the video. If that footage ever got out, it would be a huge setback for yoga, confirming every public suspicion that the practice, rather than being the greatest way ever devised to calm the human mind, was actually a destructive force that led to the worst possible cult-like behavior. The fact that it could simultaneously be both would be beyond the public's general comprehension. Maybe that confusion had been the *Kura* hoaxer's intent all along, but that person hadn't counted on Matt Bolster. The case was solved, but Bolster still had work. He wanted to go to the source.

Since he was already east, Bolster swung up to a sandwich shop in Eagle Rock that he liked, Dave's Chillin & Grillin, and had himself an Italian. He felt like crap afterward, but it tasted good going down. Then it was over to that Mexican coffee joint down the street on Colorado for a mocha with real Mexico City dark chocolate, and just a little mini-churro to round it out. It was all off Bolster's usual meal plan, but he felt like celebrating, even silently, even alone.

Then he swung up Mount Washington, toward Lora Powell's zendo. Lora was out front, sweeping with a homemade corn broom. Lora made these herself and sold them sometimes on Etsy, because she was crafty that way. She worked a little corner of concrete spotless.

"Hi, Matt!" she said.

"That looks done," he said.

"The sweeping is never done," she said. "I saw that you wrapped up the Ajoy case. Congratulations."

"Thanks," Bolster said, "but it's not exactly finished yet."

"How so?"

"There are still answers I need, and just one man who can give them to me."

"Ooooh, how exciting!"

"So I'm gonna need you to come stay at my place with your cat for a while."

"Well, of course," she said. "But how long is a while?"

"I'm not sure," Bolster said. "Don't make too many extra plans. Also, I'm gonna need a ride to the airport. You can keep Whitey while I'm gone."

"You still haven't said where."

"I have to go to India," Bolster said.

TWENTY-FIVE

———— o ————

B OLSTER HADN'T TRAVELED MUCH IN HIS LIFE—OREGON,
Washington, Arizona, Nevada, and a week once in Cancún
pretty much comprised the sum of his global adventuring. This
was definitely a gap that he felt acutely. He didn't buy into the
idea that you could experience the whole world even if you'd
spent your entire life in Southern California. Sure, if you read
enough food blogs, you could suss out the greatest Chinese
dumplings, drink *boba* tea made with yak's milk, or try some
huarache recipe drawn from the memory vault of an old woman
whose Mexican village had blown away during the Eisenhower
administration. But after you paid the bill, you were still only five
blocks from I-10. It didn't really count as travel if you could get
home in time to watch *Sunday Night Football*.

So beyond the fact that he'd spent 5 percent of the money he'd
made from the LAPD on a round-trip ticket to Kolkata, Bolster
was nervous about the trip. He'd made his decision quickly and
with little research, had brought no medicines other than a half
bottle of Advil, and had packed only a half dozen clean pairs of
underwear, two clean shirts, one extra pair of pants, a toothbrush
and travel-size toothpaste, his never-stamped passport, a stack
of rupees that had cost him a fortune to exchange downtown,
and a book of yoga philosophy to help him fall asleep. Bolster

bought no global data plan for his phone, and carried no maps or guidebooks. He had only one stop on his itinerary, but he had no idea where it was, how he'd get there, or where he'd stay once he arrived. This was no preplanned vacation.

The trip took fifteen hours, gate to gate. Bolster had read some articles online about doing yoga and breathing exercises while flying to help avoid jet lag, but it was clear once he got on board, that all those suggestions were useless. His attempts at *trikonasana* in the galley were met by disapproving flight-attendant glances; the only place with space enough to meditate was by the bathroom, where passengers weren't allowed to congregate, and a headstand in the aisle was simply out of the question. He didn't want to be that guy: a white yoga enthusiast on his way to the motherland, unable to keep his hobbyist enthusiasms in check. But he *was* that guy, and yoga was failing him. Unable to live or think in the present, Bolster let his mind run away with fantasies about what India would be like, whom he'd find there, and what he'd do once he found them. He was like a kid heading off to summer camp for the first time. He slept maybe three hours.

He arrived at eight thirty a.m., his eyes red and throbbing, his mouth dry, his joints feeling like rusted tin, and it wasn't exactly like he got a fresh washcloth upon arrival. The airport was grubby beyond belief, a nightmare of filthy carpets and randomly thrown-about trash, with gates dotted by poorly spaced iron seats that looked like they'd been lifted from a 1950s bus terminal, all illumined by inconsistent fluorescence that gave the whole scene a gray, stop-motion feel, like in *Hostel* or some equally seedy torture-porn flick. Even LAX, that sorrowful civic embarrassment, was better than this pit. On the long march to customs, Bolster saw a display indicating that Kolkata was slated to get a new international terminal in 2013. From the drawings, it looked like it would be fresh and clean and soaring, all angular lines; high-priced, duty-free saris; and cool blue carpet—a

Parisian architect's expansive vision of a new global future. The New India was announcing its arrival, but Old India hadn't yet met the wrecking ball. Bolster had landed a few months early.

Passport check was mercifully brief. The clerk asked Bolster why he'd come to India, and Bolster just muttered, "Business."

"What kind of business?"

"Spiritual."

That got Bolster a stamp *and* an eye roll: he was just another unshaven American hoping to solve his problems with a dip in the Ganga. Of course, if Bolster had said "police business," he probably would have gotten pulled aside. A little scorn was worth avoiding the hassle.

Outside, it was ninety-two degrees and 300 percent humidity. Bolster had felt thinner air inside a Laundromat. It smelled... *lively* out there. He staggered around briefly, his fifteen-pound backpack feeling like a sack of stones, subsumed by a mighty surge of people: business guys on their cells, families with extraordinary luggage burdens, and lanes of tiny cars belching little puffs of black smoke, like they were teenagers sneaking a cig behind the portables. It reminded him, in its heartless busyness and general indifference to sanity, of Los Angeles; only in L.A. there were no beggars to step over on the way to the cabstand. L.A. didn't have pariahs, unless you counted unemployed screenwriters.

Bolster reached a row of brightly colored pedicabs, which sat in a line like unclaimed carnival prizes. The drivers descended upon him hungrily. He threw up his hands and pointed at one, who made a loud, guttural sound, causing the rest of the drivers to shoo.

Bolster sat in the back of the pedicab, on a hard bench.

"Where you going, uncle?" asked the driver.

"Howrah," said Bolster.

"Howrah Station?"

"I don't know."

"Howrah very far. Or not very far, but you only get there on bridges. Lots of traffic."

"Just take me, please."

"Too much time and bad for my legs."

"But…"

"I take you to train station. There, you get train to Howrah Station. Thirty minutes. Easier and less rupees."

Bolster had no specific plans, and this guy seemed honest. Or maybe he just didn't feel like biking across a crowded bridge. Regardless, a train to Howrah seemed to be what the universe was offering, and when the universe offers you something, you must flow. Bolster could take the train.

"OK," he said.

"Why you going to Howrah?" the driver asked.

"Business," said Bolster.

"Nobody goes to Howrah," the driver said, "unless they have to."

The train to Howrah crawled through concrete and scrub trees lining Kolkata's middle-class suburbs, though at some point they did pass a spectacular cantilevered bridge that was one of the most beautiful Bolster had seen. It was so crowded on the train that Bolster felt like he was getting compressed into a human terrine. He wondered: Who were all these people? Why were they here? Where were they going at ten a.m.? How on earth did they not kill one another all the time every day? *No wonder yoga had emerged from India*, he thought. *They needed it here.*

After about thirty minutes, they arrived at Howrah Station, an impressive, block-long, redbrick leftover from the Raj, vast and clean on the inside and full of brightly colored shops. Bolster noticed quite a few people, who by their dress and possessions appeared to be middle-class by US standards, sleeping on the floor of the station on top of elaborately patterned blankets. He would have taken a cell-phone picture of this curiosity, but he believed that, other than maybe a topless drunk girl at a rock festival, other people's lives were off limits to his lame attempts at photography. The world wasn't his personal album. He preferred to let scenes drift by, as if they were from a half-remembered film.

Outside, the air was foul and the streets crowded. Howrah's landscape seemingly offered nothing but traffic and industrial smoke. Bolster knew lots of beautiful yoga people who traveled to special yoga retreats in Bali and Costa Rica to get in touch with their essences and to feel the vibrating hum of the earth. But yoga as they currently knew it had actually been born here, in the Indian equivalent of 1880s Newcastle. Bolster noted the irony.

At the station, Bolster found a cab and asked the driver to take him to the botanic garden. It was about eight kilometers away, a trip that took fewer than twenty minutes and didn't cost particularly much. Near the entrance, he bought a bottle of water and a couple of samosas from a street vendor and sat on a bench, gulping hungrily. His head felt like it was full of bees. The world appeared hazy, an unreal abstraction, yet it was very real: the bench, the food, and Bolster, sitting there in India, swatting away flies.

When Bolster finished, he paid his admission and went inside the park. This being a workday, there were few other visitors; most tourists in this part of the world wisely stayed on the other side of the river. Bolster walked the shadeless path, sweating through his shirt. On either side of him were long expanses of grass that were colored a hideous greenish-brown from being subjected to endless baking under the sun, mixing with air that was mostly soot, and being accented by downpours strong enough to make Shiva himself weep for mercy. After fifteen minutes or so of walking, Bolster turned a corner, and there it sat in all its magnificence, four acres across and a whole kilometer in circumference: the Great Banyan.

As Bolster approached the banyan tree, it looked like a grove, or a series of groves. But as he neared the entrance, he realized these were all branches of the same tree, a great family claiming its estate. *This tree must be a thousand years old*, Bolster thought. In fact, it was about 250 years old, a toddler compared with some California redwoods, but banyans spread fast and long, given the opportunity.

Under the canopy, it was at least ten degrees cooler. Bolster welcomed the relief from the sun's relentless assault. He walked for many minutes until he reached what appeared to be the center of the banyan colony. There sat a large clearing in the middle. In the 1920s, lightning had struck the Great Banyan and the tree had become diseased. Provincial officials had cut out the middle of the tree to save the rest. At the center of the banyan's decayed heart, Bolster could see, sat a man. Bolster drew closer. The man wore nothing but a simple loincloth. He sat there, legs crossed, hands resting gently on his knees, meditating, looking implacably serene. Bolster breathed in and tried to keep his head as clear as possible. He approached, only about twenty feet away now, and he could see that the man was as thin as a skeleton and had a long white beard and even longer white hair. He was very, very old, as old as anyone Bolster had ever seen.

"Excuse me?" Bolster said.

The old man opened his eyes, and suddenly Bolster knew for sure who he was.

Sri Charan Jindra.

TWENTY-SIX

———— o ————

"**I**T'S YOU," BOLSTER SAID.

"It is," Sri Charan said.

"How old *are* you?"

"I'm not certain," said Sri Charan. "It's been many years since anyone cared, including me. Very old, though."

"I've come from America…"

"I could tell."

"How?"

"Because of your accent. And because you're Caucasian. And very much sweating."

The old man unnerved Bolster with his calmness, his matter-of-factness, and his absolute stillness. Bolster could question anybody in any circumstance, but this guy seemed to have an advantage. He pressed.

"I've come from America because I'm investigating the death of Ajoy Chaterjee."

"Poor, deluded Ajoy," Sri Charan said.

"Yes."

"You are Matt Bolster, then."

Bolster was, understandably, stunned.

"How did you hear about me?"

"I go to the Internet café twice a week to read the news and check for shopping deals on Amazon India."

"Oh."

"I saw the news of Ajoy's death, so I did a Google search and found Suzie Hahn's blog. You weren't in the police reports, but she was very comprehensive. I figured if anyone from America would seek me out, it would be you."

"Here I am," Bolster said.

"Here you are."

"So why did you kill Ajoy Chaterjee?" Bolster asked.

"I did no such thing," said Sri Charan. "Ajoy killed himself."

"But it was you who gave him the idea."

"He had no ideas of his own," said Sri Charan. "Someone had to give him some."

Here we go, Bolster thought.

"What do you mean?" Bolster asked.

"I taught Ajoy this 'Sequence' many years ago because I knew that people in the West weren't ready to live like true yogis. For many years, it seemed like Ajoy was teaching it right, but then money got involved and he became greedy. It perverted from his original intent."

"So what do you care?" Bolster said. "That happens all the time with yoga. As long as one still carries on the true teachings oneself, a warped interpretation shouldn't be a concern."

"Well," said Sri Charan, "I would like to have received *some* acknowledgment."

"But Ajoy *did* acknowledge you. He talked about you all the time. There were photos of you up in all his studios. He respected his lineage."

"A plane ticket to the United States would have been nice," said Sri Charan. "I always wanted to see the Pacific Ocean. And Disneyland."

Now Sir Charan was sounding like a Jewish grandmother. *You never call, you never write…*

"That's why you kept haranguing him? You know that he took those letters and videos very seriously."

Sri Charan sighed.

"Ajoy was a great disappointment to me in many ways," he said. "He never realized his great promise."

"I would say he *more* than realized it," Bolster said. "He was the wealthiest and most successful yoga teacher in the world."

"What are wealth and success when people are faced with the cosmic winds of eternity?" said Sri Charan. "All our great works are dust motes floating in the all-seeing light of pure awareness."

Yeah, yeah, Bolster thought.

"That's fine," he said. "Maybe Ajoy charged too much for his teacher trainings. But not everyone gets to train in a park with a master like you. Or, in your case, learn yoga in a secluded Himalayan cave."

"I didn't study yoga in a Himalayan cave."

"What?"

"I grew up during the Raj. We exercised so we could become strong and overthrow the British. We did the poses in our local gymnasium both before and after school. As for meditation, I learned it from my grandfather, who sat silently every night for twenty minutes after brushing his teeth."

"So it's all a lie," Bolster said.

"More or less," said Sri Charan.

"And the Sequence?"

"How do you say it in the West? I 'pulled it out of my ass'? Well, I did. Yoga as you comprehend it came straight out of my old Indian ass."

Sri Charan gave a little chuckle.

"It really is quite a prank," he said. "All these millions of people, stretching and grinding away, thinking they're going to achieve enlightenment, when in reality they're just doing poses from an old British physical culture textbook while reciting half-formed prayers to minor Hindu deities."

"But yoga must work in some way," Bolster said. "Look at you."

"I don't eat meat, gently exercise two hours a day, have few possessions, and meditate constantly," Sri Charan said. "Also, both my grandmothers lived past the age of one hundred. There may be some wisdom to take from what you all call my 'lifestyle,' but it's not necessarily yoga."

"Then why did you tell Ajoy to bring yoga to the West?"

"It was a game," Sri Charan said.

"A game? You ruined that man's life!"

"It's not my fault he didn't figure out the rules. And he was selfish, and spoiled, and venal. He *did* pervert the practice. He became stupid."

"He was human," Bolster said.

"Exactly."

"And who are you to judge him, or any of us?"

"I'm no one. Just an old man who sits under a tree."

Bolster found himself getting very frustrated with this inscrutable fraud.

"Ajoy died doing a ritual called the *Anihatra Kura*," Bolster said. "Did you make that up as well?"

"Of course," said Sri Charan. "I cobbled together a bunch of rituals from old Tantric texts—none of which were meant to be taken seriously—put them on old-looking paper, and mailed them to Ajoy."

"And by that point, he was too broken-down to realize it was fake."

"I suppose," said Sri Charan, "though I had no way of knowing whether he was broken down or not. I was all alone here, by myself."

Would it kill you to send a postcard once in a while?

"He did the whole *Anihatra Kura*," Bolster said. "Every last gory little detail, as you outlined."

"I'm not responsible for Ajoy's moral weaknesses," Sri Charan said. "He did what he did. I merely provided a lifetime of suggestions. He failed the test."

"You killed him!" Bolster said.

Sri Charan shrugged. Bolster loathed indifference. He slapped the old man across the face, hard. Sri Charan recoiled a bit, but then quickly returned to his seated passivity.

"Did hitting me make you feel better?" Sri Charan asked.

"A little," Bolster said.

It actually did, because he knew that was all the justice he was going to get. No legal system in the world would extradite a centenarian for goading a yoga teacher into suicide by mailing him false scripture. The Constitution simply didn't go that far.

"We are born alone, Mr. Bolster," said Sri Charan, "and we die alone. No amount of so-called wisdom can keep us from the void."

"Thanks for the tip," Bolster said.

"Can I help you with anything else?" the old man asked.

"Maybe a suggestion for someplace to stay around here."

"There are many nice hotels in Kolkata," said Sri Charan. "Don't stay in Howrah. This town is a dump."

Bolster turned and walked away. He didn't look back. For all he cared, the founder of modern yoga could sit there under the great tree, alone with his profound thoughts, for the rest of eternity.

TWENTY-SEVEN

○

BOLSTER WRITHED ON THE BED OF HIS MIDPRICED CITY hotel, pale and sweaty and alone, his gut twisting in agony. The pains had started soon after he'd checked in and had barely let up at all since. He'd gone through all his Advil on the first day, and all his toilet paper on the third. Every few hours, a timid-looking housekeeper brought him a fresh bottle of water. He took it from her if he could make it to the door. Otherwise, she just left it outside until he could get up to fetch it himself, which sometimes took a couple of hours.

Kolkata. Shit. I'm still only in Kolkata.

A great evil had grabbed hold of Bolster, and he felt that he was dying. The time that he'd spent posing and sitting and resting, learning Sanskrit, contemplating life's mysteries, studying human anatomy, twisting, breathing rhythmically, chanting mantra, practicing absurd rituals with candles, offering himself up to something higher: it had all been a grand lie. In his fever, he saw the old man sitting there under the Great Banyan, pointing and laughing at him. If he somehow emerged from this death-room, Bolster vowed to kill the man, no matter how old.

He had a vision of a great arena, ringed by flame. Since this was a vision, the arena had no advertising. It was eternal and pure. All around the arena, Bolster could see, on risers, his yoga students, his yoga teachers, and his yoga friends. Everyone from the Ajoy case was there as well: Slim, Suzie Hahn, Martha Wickman, Lora Powell, Chelsea Shell, Greg Vining, Casey Anderson, Marcus Robinson and all his thugs, dead or alive, even Martinez, sitting there with his arms crossed, looked bored as usual by all this yoga shit. In the center of the ring sat Ajoy Chaterjee, in his loincloth, on his throne, looking resplendent and pure and undamaged. Bolster stood to one side of him, wearing nothing but yoga shorts, which was surprising because he never practiced shirtless, and to the other, there was Sri Charan, smirking and self-confident. Ajoy raised a hand as if to make a decree. Bolster suddenly knew that he was meant to do battle with Sri Charan. But which side did he represent? Was his cause just, or was he a usurper?

"You will battle until you are done," Ajoy said, "and the winner will control the soul of yoga."

The crowd sat in silent judgment, except for Suzie Hahn, who was excitedly taking notes. Bolster wasn't exactly sure what to do. Yoga wasn't a martial art like hapkido or kung fu, at least not as he'd learned it. There were no blocking or striking poses. He did all he knew, raising his arms overhead, inhaling, turning his gaze upward, and then swan-diving forward into a deep bend, making sure not to lock his knees and that his sacrum tilted along with his spine. Inhaling, Bolster lifted his perineum, activating the mystical *mula bandha*, drew up into a tabletop, folded in, and jumped back into *chaturanga dandasana*.

On his hotel bed, Bolster writhed, trying to break his fevered hallucination. But he couldn't. He was in the grip of madness, and in that madness, he was experiencing the worst kind of yoga hell: the *ashtanga* primary series.

The arena had a dirt floor, and Bolster was soon blowing up dust with his sun salutations. He had to focus, or he'd get hurt;

it was just his breath and his *drishti*, a tight gaze on a fixed point in the distance. He jumped back and floated forward, fighting for yoga as hard as he could, with maximum effort, dipping into triangle and revolved triangle, bowing forward and bending back (but mostly forward), taking his warrior postures, every muscle and sinew straining, every cell in his body bathing in the fresh oxygen carried on the chariot of his breath. Bolster hit the ground, and it didn't get any easier. The arena was totally silent, save the sound of his deep *ujjayi* breathing. He heard nothing else as he bent and twisted and lifted, going for the full bind, sweating like a wild horse. Nothing mattered but the pose in the present moment.

It went on like this forever, seemingly. Bolster did *navasana*, boat pose, for five deep breaths, balancing on his sit bones, folding lotus, lifting up, and then drifting back into boat again, doing this five times. He performed a full embryo, turning clockwise while folded up like a fetus, the sweat and the dirt merging to cake his back with mud. Bolster was exhausted, but he still had to do the finishing poses. It was a full series of back bends, plus a headstand and the grueling shoulder-stand series, a restorative fish pose, and finally, mercifully, ten breaths in seated meditation before lifting up for ten long breaths, legs crossed in lotus, arms straining, gaze fixed, the crowd silent, everyone sitting in judgment, and one last long jump back before *savasana*.

Bolster lay there, feeling the *prana* flowing freely through his body, seeking the rest beyond rest. Then he realized that for nearly two hours, while he'd been whipping and flailing around the arena like a hyper gymnast, Sri Charan had been sitting calmly, legs crossed, hands resting on his knees, silently mocking Bolster with his stillness. Now he rose, walked over to Bolster, and sat back down again, this time on Bolster's chest. Bolster took the load at first; at this point, the old man couldn't weigh more than one hundred pounds. But gradually, he realized that he was having trouble breathing, and not just in his hallucination. He began to gasp, and to claw at the air.

"How's your *pranayama* practice now, Mr. Bolster?" Sri Charan asked, and chuckled cruelly.

Bolster couldn't reply; he could only wheeze as he felt the old man grow heavier and heavier, crushing him with his leathery bones. The crowd shuffled restlessly while Suzie Hahn took notes.

"You're a fool to believe in yoga," said the old man. "It has no purpose. Enlightenment is impossible. Only death awaits us all."

Bolster felt the light going from his eyes, the soul draining from his body. Then, from Ajoy's throne, he heard, "*Enough!*"

Sri Charan turned toward his master pupil.

"Have I upset the baby?" he said.

"Yoga helps people," Ajoy said. "It is *good!*"

"Tell that to the disciples you abandoned."

"I never abandoned them. I was with them until I died."

"And yoga died with you," said Sri Charan.

"No," said Ajoy Chaterjee. "It died with *you.*"

Ajoy stepped off his throne, walked over to Sri Charan, and twisted his neck. The old man struggled, was laughing even, but he wasn't as strong as his pupil. Bolster heard a sickening *crack*, and then Sri Charan's head lay limp. As the guru's seated body slid off his chest, Bolster felt air return to his lungs.

Bolster awoke in his hotel room with a huge gasp. Then the room was silent, save the whirring of a wall-mounted air conditioner. The sheets were soaked and smelled deeply sour. It was night. Bolster sat up, turned on a light, and looked at himself in a wall mirror. He'd lost twenty pounds and looked like a forgotten refugee, or a shipwreck survivor. But he was alive, and he felt hungry.

The next morning, Bolster showered, ate breakfast, and went back to the botanic garden. Sri Charan had tipped over where he sat, his face drawn into a sad grimace. Bolster nudged the old man with his foot, just to make sure, but Sri Charan didn't move.

Walking back to the entrance, Bolster found a security guard. "Dead yogi under the banyan tree," he said.

EPILOGUE

○

BOLSTER TRAVELED NORTH, TAKING A TRAIN UP TO LUCKNOW and then a random series of rickety buses, until he reached the ashram. He'd found it online, but it wasn't some trendy spiritual-healing center frequented by Western enlightenment tourists. Bolster didn't want to eat, pray, or love. All he wanted was to sit in silence, and at this place, essentially three rooms on a rural road, he found it—just him, a couple of German hippies, and a portly middle-aged woman who had some cushions and a method and access to that most precious commodity of all: silence. In the mornings, Bolster sat for three hours, punctuated only by short bouts of walking meditation, head bowed, hands folded like the bride of Frankenstein. Then he had a simple vegetarian lunch, followed by more sitting. At three thirty p.m., they'd drink home-brewed tea and then he'd be free to read or do *asana* or hike in the surrounding hills for a few hours, until dinner and another hour of sitting before bed. There were a few light chores, like dishes and sweeping. He did this every day for a month, and didn't speak a word.

Yoga mattered to him, as much as it ever had. This became clear. Its meaning could get gummed up by ego and fashion and all manner of silliness, but such was the way of the world. It threw up distractions, almost for its own amusement, to keep you from realizing true reality as it was: immutable, glorious, and unchanging. The world is a magnificent tapestry of celebration and suffering, stupidity and insight, struggle and freedom, darkness and light, and it's our job to live in it with as much awareness as we can muster during the short time that we're blessed to have. Bolster knew this now. His body and mind filled with coolness and joy. He'd been through the mill and still had about forty grand left in the bank. No one could stop the Matt Bolster Express now.

Two months after he'd left, Bolster flew home. Lora picked him up at the airport. She'd brought Charlemagne with her. The cat didn't seem happy.

"He'd rather be watching TV," Bolster said.

Lora gave him a kiss on the cheek.

"It's good to see you, Matt," she said. "You've been missed."

He'd done some missing himself. As soon as he got home, Bolster loaded up the vaporizer and took a huge drag, feeling the *sativa* spark his synapses almost immediately. Then he put out the call: *Meet at my place, Saturday morning, 10 a.m. Bring a mat. Don't be late.*

They all came: Lora Powell and Suzie Hahn. Slim, Martha Wickman. A few of his favorite students. Chelsea Shell wasn't there. He hadn't invited her. But Martinez came, though he brought beer instead of a yoga mat.

"Welcome home, Bolster," Slim said.

They sat around and chatted for a while. Someone sparked a joint. Good weed, good friends, and good weather abounded. Bolster reveled in all that mattered to him. Only one thing was missing.

After half an hour, he starting moving his furniture to the sides of the room, creating enough space for ten people, maybe more, to spread out comfortably. It was ten thirty in the morning, the best time of day to practice. Bolster smiled.

"Shut up, people," he said. "Let's do some yoga."

ACKNOWLEDGMENTS

———— o ————

THANKS TO COURTNEY MILLER, JEFF BELLE, KRISTI Coulter, and the whole team at Amazon Publishing and Thomas & Mercer for their hard work and their faith in my ability to produce a novel on deadline. Also thanks to Daniel Greenberg and the Levine Greenberg team, and to The Smiley Group, LLC. Let's do it again sometime.

ABOUT THE AUTHOR

———— o ————

N EAL POLLACK WAS BORN IN MEMPHIS, TENNESSEE, BUT
spent most of his childhood in Arizona. After graduating
from Northwestern University's Medill School of Journa-lism, he
worked as a staff writer at the *Chicago Reader.* His first book, *The
Neal Pollack Anthology of American Literature*, was published in
2000, becoming an (almost) instant cult classic. His debut novel,
Never Mind the Pollacks, hit shelves in 2003, and was shamelessly
promoted by his band, The Neal Pollack Invasion. In 2007, he
published *Alternadad*, a best-selling memoir that was optioned
for film and television and led to a miserable subcareer as a daddy
blogger. In 2010 Pollack became a certified yoga teacher and published *Stretch*, a nonfiction account of his adventures in American
yoga culture. He has contributed to the *New York Times*, *Wired*,
Slate, *Yoga Journal*, and *Vanity Fair*, among many other publica-
tions, and has published crime fiction in numerous anthologies.
Thomas & Mercer published his historical noir novel *Jewball* in
March 2012. He and his wife, the painter Regina Allen, live with
their son in Austin, Texas.

Kindle *Serials*

THIS BOOK WAS ORIGINALLY RELEASED IN EPISODES AS A Kindle Serial. Kindle Serials launched in 2012 as a new way to experience serialized books. Kindle Serials allow readers to enjoy the story as the author creates it, purchasing once and receiving all existing episodes immediately, followed by future episodes as they are published. To find out more about Kindle Serials and to see the current selection of Serials titles, visit www.amazon.com/kindleserials.

Printed in Great Britain
by Amazon